New Nails and a Nasty Nightmare

A Sunny Cove Cozy Mystery

By

Ava Zuma

ISBN: 9798694963138
Imprint: Independently Published

Other books in the Sunny Cove Series

Makeup and Mayhem

Eyebrows and Evil Looks

New Nails and a Nasty Nightmare

A

Sunny Cove

COZY MYSTERY

Book Three

1

Celia Dube enjoyed humming a happy song in the morning. She sometimes believed she gave the chirping birds a run for their money as she hummed. It energized her and set the tone for her day. Today, she was in tune with Miriam Makeba's famous song 'Pata Pata' as she hummed and danced on her bedroom balcony. This song brought with it a mixture of memories; which included joyful and painful moments.

She paused briefly to watch the ocean waters ahead of her slap against the rocks and sandy beach. This view was one of the reasons she had moved to Sunshine Cove with her late husband, Trevor. When they had seen this house and what it had to offer, there was no going back. This was where they'd raise a family. She loved the fact that she was just fifteen minutes away from the beach and the fine sand. In the midst of her hectic days, these moments made it worthwhile.

They used to hum together. It wasn't his type of

thing at first. He was an army man, the type who was used to bellowing out orders. To him silence or subtle hums were meant for stealth, not joyful expression. Once he was converted, they would dance together on that very balcony, welcoming new days when he was home, or dancing under the stars.

"Cece, are you planning to leave or what?" a shrill voice shouted from below. Celia stopped her humming to look down at the speaker. It was her mother, Audrey Matinise and she didn't look too happy.

"I'm taking a break, Ma!" Celia replied.

"I thought you're supposed to be delivering some orders this morning?"

"Like I said, I'm taking a break before I finish up then head out."

"You're taking breaks and the day hasn't even started yet. What will happen by midday?" Audrey said.

Celia laughed. Often, the smallest pleasures rattled her mother. She was staying with them for the next couple of days and was always a big help. Celia had two boys to raise, and they were a handful as they were growing so fast. Motherly duties aside, Celia needed short breaks every now and then.

It had been an intense couple of days promoting a new line of Maven beauty products. As the lead Maven beauty consultant in Sunshine Cove, Celia had to ensure each of the new products gained traction in the market.

Sunshine Cove was your typical small coastal suburban town, full of tourists in shorts walking the streets, visiting gift shops, enjoying the cuisine at local seafood restaurants, wearing colorful casual wear and keeping a relaxed pace to life.

Celia knew her market and that one-on-one interactions with her clients helped to sell her products.

That's where Celia always shone. She had impeccable charming skills that won over even the toughest of clients. Although her years of experience gave her an edge over her competition, it was still a lot of work. Song and dance helped her fight the burnout that sought to slow down her endeavors.

She had several orders to make that day, and she wasn't done prepping the delivery packs. She worked from home, with one of the bedrooms specially converted to house weekly deliveries of stock that she received from the city headquarters. She knew she would have to give up the bedroom when her two sons got older. For now, it was there to build up funds for their future. If Trevor was still alive, he'd have approved.

She was finishing the last packs when her mother came in.

"Cece, have you seen the little dinosaur man?" her mother asked with her usual quizzical expression.

Although she was in her fifties, Audrey Matinise looked younger than her years. She claimed that spending time with her two grandsons was the secret to her renewed youthfulness, and Celia wasn't keen to argue with that.

"You can't use the Dinosaur Man anymore to charm the kids. It's been there for the last four years," Celia said.

"As the chief organizer of your kids' birthday parties, I know what works for them and what doesn't. Dinosaur Man is a popular feature," Audrey insisted.

Celia wasn't convinced. The Dinosaur Man was a life-size dinosaur head outfit with arms. You put it on and it covered the head, arms, shoulders and half the torso. The wearer became half human, half dinosaur. Admittedly, the boys loved it. But Celia felt it was time for a change.

"Have you considered that maybe the Dinosaur Man

wants to retire?"

Audrey wasn't taking the bait.

"Have you seen it?" she asked.

"No, I haven't seen it. Even if I had, I wouldn't tell you where it was," Celia replied.

"Now why would you do something like that?" Audrey asked.

"I know why you're looking for it. You do this every year, Ma."

"What are you talking about?" Audrey asked.

"Stop acting all innocent. We're not doing that this year. We're celebrating James' birthday in a whole new way," Celia said emphatically.

"But I always make it a little different every year," Audrey said.

"It doesn't matter if you buy him a new set of clothes or a new toy or bake a different cake. For Frank, the main attraction is always the little dinosaur because you know he loves dinosaurs. But we need to show him a different experience this time, don't you think?" Celia asked.

"He's still a child. He has plenty of time to learn about those other things."

"He's turning eight in a few days. This is the best time to let his young, curious brain absorb every bit of knowledge about things. Let's show him a new side of Sunshine Cove," Celia said.
"Well, it just sounds to me like you're being a party pooper," Audrey remarked.

"What? Hear me out. I don't mind you planning the birthdays like you always have. But please, can you try something different this time?" Celia pleaded.

Audrey shook her head.

"Come on, Ma, you must have a few new ideas," Celia prodded.

"I can't promise anything, but I will give it some thought," Audrey replied as she left the room.

Celia smiled to herself. She knew this wasn't going to be a walk in the park for her mother but she was curious to see how it would go.

Celia's favorite coffee house, The Pier, was bought out recently and given a full facelift. Where formerly it had a finish similar to your regular city coffee shop with walls full of posters and flashy colors, the restaurant was now more homely. It had dark wood paneling inside and out that gave it that cozy feel. It's new owner, Festo Tshabalala, was a charming man. Stout and energetic, he wore smart casual suits and was always smiling at clients when they walked in. Celia had a date with Melanie Dawes, one of her great friends. Melanie was a librarian with a vibrant personality, and Celia liked her curious nature. They met at least twice every week to connect and unwind from their busy schedules.

"Enjoying your visit, ladies?" he asked Celia and Melanie who were seated in one of the plush booths.

"We would be if our order was already here," Celia replied with a smile.

As if on cue, the waiter arrived with a loaded tray in hand. He served them their piping hot caramel tea and café mocha with two slices of carrot cake each.

"You were saying?" Festo asked, knowing he now had the upper hand.

"Yes, sir! We're now officially enjoying this!" Melanie replied. They all laughed.

"That's what I like to hear. If you need anything else, don't hesitate to let my people know," he replied, and moved to the next table.

"I'm going to fall in love with this place," Celia mused

before she took a sip of the caramel tea.
"You and me both," Melanie replied. "So I have regular news and not so regular news that I want to share with you. Which do you want to hear first?"

Celia raised her eyebrows quizzically.

"Give me the regular news," Celia replied.

"Okay, here we go," Melanie said, taking a deep breath, "I'm opening a business."

"Are you serious?" Celia asked.

"Of course, I am. Are you saying that I don't look like a business owner?" Melanie asked.

"I didn't say that. I'm just surprised that's all. I mean, your passion and experience is centered around the library and I never pictured you in another place."

"You just admitted that I don't look like a business owner," Melanie replied.

"Oh, I did? I take it back. I'm sorry," she apologized.

"It's fine. Well, I can be full of surprises so don't be fooled," she said with confidence.
"I'll take your word for it. Tell me more about this new business."

"It's a nail parlor on Main Street. I'm talking manicures, pedicures and everything in between."

"A nail parlor? Wow, this keeps getting better. You know I'm in the beauty products business and you didn't tell me?" Celia protested.

"Hey, go easy on me! I'm telling you now, am I not?"

Celia shook her head.

"Anyway, the reason I'm telling you this is because I'm going to have a soft launch. Consider this an official invitation," Melanie said.

"Okay, sounds good. Tell me the date and I'll rearrange my schedule. I think I'll even come with a friend or two. Is that okay?" Celia asked.

"Sure! Just let me know who it is."

"Chloe Matthews. She's crazy about nails."

"Ah, our Chloe? Yeah, she's great company. The launch is tomorrow. You'll make it?" Melanie asked.

"Sure. Let me text Chloe right now," Celia said as she took out her phone, "I still can't believe you kept this bubbling under the surface all this time."

"I told you I was full of surprises," Melanie replied.

The two women laughed.

Celia was impressed. She admired her friend's new venture but wondered if she was biting off more than she could chew. She could tell it was not going to be a regular week.

2

It was a warm evening made for a night out, Celia thought as she walked down Main Street. Up ahead, she could see her destination.

The Afrostar Nail Parlor had a sizeable window front made of reinforced glass. While most of the upper part was clear such that you could see into the establishment, the lower sections of the window front had colorful stickers of two beautiful models showing immaculately done nails. Stylish and clean, it was slightly above the level of the other shops on Main Street.

It also had a neon sign in cursive font and gold lettering that had not come on although darkness had already fallen. Perhaps Melanie and her business partner didn't want to attract much attention from passers-by, Celia mused.

At the entrance, a large man in a tan suit confirmed her name was on the guest list and ushered her in.

Inside, she was one of ten people present. Soft jazz music by Hugh Masekela filtered through the room.

The space was all white, with large mirrors along the longest walls. In front of the mirrors were customized leather seats for the customers. Next to each seat was a padded carpet. On the ceiling were miniature soft lights, which complemented the larger ones along the walls. It felt luxurious without looking out of reach.

"You look amazing," Melanie exclaimed as she walked towards Celia. Melanie was dressed in a long black and white satin dress that shimmered in the light.

"Why, thank you," Celia replied, gushing with pride. "It was a gift from a good client that I have never worn."

It was a mustard yellow evening dress with colorful patterns around her neck inspired by the Ndebele Isigolwani neck ring. She loved it. She'd never worn it because it stood out, and Celia usually liked blending into the background. Tonight was an exception.

"You didn't have to outshine us," Melanie said teasingly.

"Well, you said that you're launching your first business venture, and there was no way I was going to come here in anything less," Celia replied with a smile.

"Are you going to check mine out as well or the compliments are just reserved for Cece?" Chloe Matthews asked. She wore a fitting gray dress that accentuated her figure with black heels.

Melanie laughed.

"I was coming to you, be patient!" Melanie said, "You know that between the three of us you're always pulling out the classiest looks. You have not disappointed!"

Chloe did a little twirl. As the daughter of the clothing magnate Ezra Matthews, she was expected to look stylish. She did occasionally strut her stuff at events, but she loved blending in without the tag of a wealthy man's daughter. Her down-to-earth and relatable qualities were what endeared her to Celia. Over the past two years, they had built a great friendship where they could be open with each other.

"Of course, I haven't! I'm not here to attend. I'm here to enjoy the launch of what will be the best nail parlor in Sunny Cove," Chloe said.

"Amen! Thanks for your support Chloe. We're just about to start. We're waiting for two more people,"

Melanie said.

"You already have a decent crowd," Celia remarked as she scanned the room. "That fella catches my interest. Was he on your guest list or your business partner's?"

Melanie turned to see who Celia was referring to. It was a muscular man in a grey striped suit and slick hair. He looked polished, but seemed like a man who wouldn't be afraid to roll his sleeves and get his hands dirty.

"Both of ours," Melanie replied, "He's one of our big investors."

"Hmm. There's something about him I can't put a finger on," Celia replied.

"One day I'll tell you the story," Melanie said, "for now I have to go and open this event."

"Actually, I'll do that for you," a woman dressed in a silk dress said. She smiled and gave Melanie a casual wave as she walked up to the front where a simple glass stand was waiting.

"Who on earth is that?" Chloe asked.

"That, my friends, is Charlize Langa. My business partner," Melanie replied.

The music faded away. Charlize tapped a wine glass with a pen, producing that distinct clinking sound. The murmurs stopped and everyone turned to her.

"Esteemed guests, ladies and gentlemen. We are happy to have you here as our first visitors. We hope many more will walk through those doors for the next couple of years. My name is Charlize Langa. Some of you know me as an entrepreneur, business builder, PR strategist, and fixer. If you've been in the business circles in Sunshine Cove for the past five years then you have met me using one of those titles. I have them because I am a go-getter and I assure you we are going to make this nail parlor the best in town."

The guests clapped fervently. Celia nodded as she clapped. She had heard of Charlize, but didn't know much about her.

"Let me introduce to you my business partner who will say a few words before we get to the next bit of our program. Welcome, Melanie Dawes."

Charlize led the clapping as Melanie gracefully walked to the front.

"Thank you very much Charlize for the introduction. I'm not one to talk in public, but I have to show my appreciation. My gratitude goes to each one of you for supporting us this evening. We are hoping to form long-term relationships with you. I'm a librarian by profession but a business administrator by education. I have revamped and managed an institution, built a loyal community and my visionary mindset compliments Charlize's fantastic resume. Thank you and enjoy your evening," Melanie said with a broad smile.

The claps and cheers erupted as Melanie stepped back from the podium.

"Thank you, Melanie!" Charlize began, "I'm proud to count on you and I really appreciate the fact that you value our partnership. Now this wasn't meant to be a formal evening full of long speeches and boring anecdotes. We're here to celebrate! So, let's kick up the music, pass around the finger foods, have some wine and enjoy. Please don't dance too much. The floor might be slippery – and a little expensive."

Charlize gave a cheeky wink as the guests laughed. The music returned, louder than before. Melanie walked back to where Celia and Chloe stood.

"That was beautiful," Celia said.

"Thanks, guys," Melanie replied.

"So why are you starting this business?" Celia asked.

"Well, its always been in the works. I can't just rely on one source of income. I need to fast track some of my goals. So here I am, diversifying my income," Melanie replied.

"Smart move," Chloe said.

An usher brought a platter full of steaming lamb sosaties, kebabs held on wooden skewers. It wasn't often you would find these at an event that wasn't a local backyard barbeque. They each grabbed one and dug in.

"Why the small splash?" Celia asked in between bites.

"What do you mean?" Melanie replied.

"Was it your idea to keep the launch small?"

"It wasn't. I believe in strong starts and building awareness as early as possible. Charlize had a different opinion and so we went with that," Melanie replied.

Just then, Melanie frowned. Celia followed her gaze, landing on a woman in a red dress with light tiger-paw patterns.

"What's going on?" Celia asked.

"I didn't expect to see her here," Melanie replied.

"Who is she?"

"I only know her first name. Patricia. She's the competition."

"Why would you invite your competition?" Celia asked.

"It's one of Charlize's philosophical stances. 'Know your friends but keep your potential enemies closer,' she likes to say," Melanie replied.

"That's a bold move," Chloe said.

"It's more arrogant, actually," Celia remarked.

"Well, I'll let Charlize handle it. I'm picking my fights tonight," Melanie said.

"And are you ok with that?" Celia asked.

Melanie shrugged.

"It will do for now. I just want us to focus on making it the best nail parlor this side of town. We have the next two months to do that," Melanie replied.

"Two months, you say?" Celia asked, "You're quite ambitious."

"Well Charlize and I have some pretty solid plans that we hope will come together."

"Enough about business! We need to catch up away from this work environment. It's been a while!" Chloe said.

"It sure has," Melanie agreed.

"You're not planning anything crazy, right?" Celia asked.

"Not really. Or even better, we could set up blind dates for each other," Chloe replied.

"Did you say blind dates?" Celia asked.

"Why not? I haven't heard a lot about you and Detective Bill recently. What happened?" Chloe asked with a wink. Melanie smiled.

 "That's not going to be discussed here," Celia replied, her cheeks reddening.

"Chloe is onto something here. What's the latest on the handsome detective? You two had some amazing chemistry," Melanie said.

"I remember the sparks," Chloe chimed in.

"That were destined to be flames," Melanie added

with a cheeky grin.

"Melanie, you of all people should be the last one talking about my dating life. Yours has been as barren as the desert for the last couple of months," Celia said.

"So, it sounds like all of us need a little excitement in our love lives," Chloe said. "I think I should find matches for each of us."

 "Count me out because I'm not interested," Celia said.

"There's no way we are going to do it and leave you behind," Chloe insisted.

"Come on, Cece. Just a harmless night and we can each share our experiences after our dates. Lord knows I need an entertaining one," Melanie said.

"Moving on swiftly, you do remember that I supply beauty products, right?" Celia asked. "I have a few products in our line that could suit your establishment."

"Yeah, sure. Actually, I wanted to introduce you to Charlize," Melanie turned her head and signaled Charlize to come over.

Charlize excused herself from the group she was

talking to and walked over to the three women.

"I hope you are enjoying the launch under Melanie's watch," Charlize said with a warm smile.
"She's doing an amazing job," Celia replied, returning the smile.

"I wanted to introduce you to my friends," Melanie said, "This is Chloe Matthews, the daughter of the man who owns the Matthews Clothing company."

"Nice to meet you, Chloe," Charlize said as she shook Chloe's hand. "I am honored to be in the presence of someone associated with a well-known and admired name in our community."

"I try to get out of the family shadow, but it finds me often. Congratulations on your launch," Chloe said.

"And then we have Celia Dube," Melanie continued, "She's a good friend of mine. We've done business deals together and organized events. She also happens to be the main distributor of the highly rated Maven beauty products."

"Glad to meet you, Celia," Charlize said. "Melanie has praised your products so much that I was even thinking of getting one for myself!"

"You definitely can. What do you need?" Celia asked.

"I'll check my dressing table and let you know in due course. I hope you'll be coming to visit us as a client?" Charlize asked.

"Actually, that's one of the reasons I wanted you to meet her," Melanie said, "She would like to explore the possibility of supplying us with some of her beauty products."

"We have an amazing line of nail varnishes, nail polishes and so on in a wide range of colors," Celia said as she handed Charlize a glossy catalogue.

Charlize slowly flipped through the catalogue as she listened.

"Our distribution network is very good, and price point for the quality you get is quite a good deal especially for new businesses," Celia added.

Charlize began flipping through the pages slowly, with very subtle nods of her head. Celia's body language training kicked in subconsciously. She watched Charlize purse her lips. She could tell that she was wrestling with the idea. Charlize then handed back the catalogue.
"I think we'll pick this up later, okay?" Charlize said.

"So, you're open to a conversation?" Melanie asked.

"I think you and I'll talk about this later. For now,

let's just enjoy the evening," Charlize said with a forced smile. She then turned and left.

"Why did that feel like a blow off?" Chloe asked.

"Because it was," Celia replied.

"Guys, it wasn't a blow off," Melanie said.

"Sure felt like one," Chloe insisted.

"You could tell from her body language," Celia said. "I think she doesn't want to do business with me."

"Listen. I'll talk to her and fix this, okay?" Melanie assured her.

Celia shrugged.

"Good luck with that. I can tell a tough cookie when I see one," Celia replied. "I'm more worried about you. Knowing your personality, Charlize might give you a tough time here."

3

"How about we get a trampoline?" Audrey asked.

Celia sighed.

"The kids are too young to be jumping up and down. What happens if they break their bones?" she said.

"You were jumping on trampolines at their age, Cece. Stop being funny," Audrey remarked.
"Ma, have you forgotten the day I jumped too high and sprained my ankle?" Celia asked.

"That was nothing! A little herbal ointment and some rooibos tea had you jumping around again the next day," Audrey said.

Celia laughed.

"Before they jump on the trampoline, I would like to show them how to do it safely. Forget the trampoline," Celia replied.

"So what are these children coming here to do?" Audrey asked in frustration. "Planning a party is supposed to be fun and I'm not enjoying it this year."

"But you are being stubborn with ideas," Celia said. "You should try the internet. There're tons of ideas there."

"None of the ideas I came across interest me," she replied.

"It's not about what interests you, but what interests the kids."

"I could say the same thing about you and the trampolines," she remarked.

"It's not the same thing, Ma. Why don't you get in touch with Mrs. Owens? She could help you plan this thing. She loves the kids and is good with events," she suggested.

Audrey frowned. Celia knew this might get spicy. Mrs. Owens was a great family friend, and when she got together with her mother, it was usually a lot of fun. However, sometimes they had serious disagreements.

"Remember you're doing it for the kids," Celia said as she planted a kiss on her mother's forehead. "See you later."

The Sunshine Cove Library looked immaculate in the afternoon sun. Its largely glass facade stood out in the midst of other older buildings.

Celia walked up to the library reception and found Melanie there, as usual. She was deeply engrossed, staring at her computer screen, which was hidden from view behind the counter.

"Hey, Mel," Celia whispered, keen not to disrupt the readers present in the space.

"Hey," Melanie replied without looking up. Celia rapped the countertop with her knuckles, startling her. Melanie shot her a look.

"Are you busy or can you have a quick chat?" she asked. Melanie's gaze softened.

"Sure, we can talk. I actually I need a break from all this. Are you willing to work part time?" Melanie asked.

"Here or at the nail parlor?"

"We can start with here. Right now. I just need a holiday or a getaway. Actually, we need to do that blind date soon," Melanie said.

"We killed that idea," Celia said dismissively.

"Come on, it will be fun," Melanie said, "Chloe thinks we should do it together."

"You mean at the same time?" Celia asked.

"Same time, same place. It will make you more comfortable. Just in case you don't like each other, we're your exit plan."

Celia shook her head.

"I am not going to join this bandwagon in a million years!" Celia insisted.

"Think about it for a minute," Melanie said as she turned back to the screen.

"I don't need to," Celia said with finality.

Melanie didn't reply. She was so engrossed in the computer screen, Celia got curious. She moved towards the side of the counter to get a better view.

"Is that the nail parlor you're looking at?" Celia asked.

"Yeah, it's a CCTV feed," Melanie replied.

"Why are you watching CCTV footage of your business from here?" Celia asked.

"I didn't realize how difficult it would be keeping up with a new business."

"Is it just the business you're keeping up with or something more?" Celia asked.

Melanie sighed.

"It's also not been easy to get Charlize to give me good updates about what's happening there. I mean, I can read the books of account and everything, but I need to know some of the things that happen when I'm not there. That detail just never comes out."

"You should get closer to the employees," Celia suggested.

"I'm working on that," she replied.

"How's it going with Charlize?" she asked.

"I'm managing. It's not a bed of roses, but I guess that's how things are when you're trying to get to grips with a new operation," Melanie replied.

"Did you talk to her about the proposal I gave?" Celia asked.

"I haven't really gotten time to do that. But I promise I'll do that later this evening, or at the latest tomorrow. Can you give me till then?"

"Of course I can, don't sweat it," Celia replied. "I think I'll be heading out now. I have one more delivery to make before I head home."

"Which direction are you headed?" Melanie asked.

"Towards the Farmer's Market."

"Which means you will be passing through Main Street. Fantastic! Can you drop this off for me?" Melanie asked as she handed over a cashbook. "We wanted one with our company logo on it."

"Sure! Should I give it to Charlize?"

"Yes, please. Just make sure you don't try to force the conversation again," Melanie teased.

"You have my word," Celia replied with a smile.

Some minutes after three in the afternoon, Celia arrived at the nail parlor. She found it busy with three clients, and the two staffers had their hands full. She could foresee they would need to hire new people to cover the demand.

She found Charlize attending to one of the clients who was waiting for their nails to dry.
Charlize walked up to her and smiled.

"Celia! What brings you here?"

"Hi, Charlize. Melanie asked me to drop off this cashbook," Celia said, handing it over.

"Thank you very much!" Charlize said.

"You're welcome."

Celia turned to leave and was about to step out when she decided to ask one of the employees a question. She walked up to Sarah.

"Hi, do you have silver nail polish?"

"No, we don't have it yet," she replied.

"So, how are you attending to clients who want it?"

Sarah shook her head. "We don't until Miss Langa brings it over."

After hearing this, Celia couldn't just leave. She

walked back to the counter where Charlize stood.

"I wanted to get my nails done but apparently you don't have silver nail polish?" Celia said.
"Who told you that?" Charlize asked.

"One of your staffers. I can bring it in tomorrow if that's okay."

"You asked one of my staffers if they have silver nail polish?"

"Yes, I happened to ask as I was walking out," Celia said.

"Well, your concern is noted. But all bookings are done by me, so this is the right place to ask." Charlize stated.

"I didn't know that. But I'm here now."

"I would take it slow if I were you," Charlize said.

"Excuse me?" Celia asked, puzzled.

"You're pushing too hard."

"Am I pushing too hard? I was simply making an observation that could gain you an extra client."

"And I've taken it under advisement. Still, you

shouldn't come into my store and start ordering us to do things for you," Charlize snapped.

"I was not ordering you to do things for me. It was a simple…"

Charlize interrupted.

"You made your proposal during the launch. You do not have to do it here when other clients are present."

"I didn't even raise my voice when I told you this. I am simply saying it would be nice of you to buy more stock. Melanie is my good friend and I would like her business to flourish even when she's not here."

"Are you trying to suggest that I don't know what I'm doing here?" Charlize asked.

Celia's phone started ringing. It was Melanie. Celia paused, then took it.

"Hey, Melanie. I delivered the cash book and…"

"Cece, I thought we agreed that you wouldn't talk to her about the deal?"

"I'm not talking to her about it."

"I can see what's happening right in front of me,"

Melanie replied.

Celia remembered Melanie had a camera feed into the shop.

"I hear you. I'm leaving now." Celia hung up and turned to Charlize. "I'm sorry for the miscommunication. I didn't mean to offend you."

"Thank you," Charlize said. She moved closer to Celia. "Just to make it clear: despite your friendship with Melanie, I am running the business. Please keep that in mind next time."

"I understand," Celia replied.

As she walked out, Celia couldn't help feeling something bad was about to happen.

4

Celia had just finished a client delivery when Melanie called.

Stuck in traffic, she was tempted to use her actual mobile phone handset to take the call. Then she remembered that she'd recently fixed the Bluetooth system in her car.

"Hey, Mel! Talk to me," Celia said.

"Where are you?" Melanie asked.

"I'm caught up in traffic on the other side of town."

"Do you have any other deliveries on your schedule?"

"Not at the moment. Are you making an order?" Celia asked, smiling.

Melanie laughed.

"I am actually calling to say that we can meet you now. If you have a moment, please pass by the nail parlor," Melanie said.

Celia smiled.

"Are you sure? Charlize is okay with this?" Celia asked.

"I wouldn't call you if I wasn't sure."

"Great! I'm on my way. Give me about half an hour to weave through this traffic."
Celia was glad.

"This product is called Coral Smooth nail polish. It's a tribute to coral reefs which are endangered but still very important to our fishing communities," Celia said confidently.

As she spoke, she handed bottles of the nail polish for Melanie and Charlize to look at. They were seated on the leather seats in the service area. Sarah and Fidel, the two employees, had been excused for their lunch break so that the three women could talk in private. Celia had fifteen minutes to make her case, and she was giving it her best shot.

"So you're telling me it's made out of coral reef?" Charlize asked as she turned the bottle. She squinted her eyes to read the ingredients.

"Coral is not one of the ingredients. I think that would be illegal!" Celia said with a laugh, "As I stated earlier, our products are made from fully organic materials and are good for the human body," she confidently replied.

"So why would you call it coral and yet it's not made out of coral reef?" Charlize asked again.
Melanie cleared her throat.

"I think what Celia was trying to say is that Maven beauty products as a company are
very environmentally conscious. So they have branded some of their products using the names of endangered species to highlight the causes behind them. I think that's good for our brand."

"Why don't you let her answer my question herself," Charlize said. Melanie frowned.

Celia was simmering with anger, wondering what she would say to Charlize that would not be disrespectful. She had a right to stand up for herself. She took in a deep breath.

"To echo what Melanie has said, Maven beauty products are fully organic and…"

"You said that already. Tell me something new," Charlize interjected.

Celia paused briefly before replying.

"We have a very good product that has won multiple international awards and you can use that angle to…"

Charlize put both her hands up. Celia stopped talking, disgusted by the gesture.

"Celia, with all due respect I am not here to listen to your company values. I'm sure they are of great benefit to your employees and shareholders. But right now I just can't see how bringing you on board is going to favor our nail parlor," Charlize said with finality.

Melanie was not amused.

"You're not giving her a chance to speak!" Melanie said.

"I've heard all I needed to hear. It doesn't suit my business," Charlize replied.

"This parlor is our business and I have a say in this conversation," Melanie exclaimed.

"And you have spoken. Need I remind you of the clause in our agreement that states we both must reach a consensus before any major decision? Nothing short of that can make us move forward,"

Charlize said.

Melanie bit her lip and went quiet, struggling to control her anger.

She exchanged a look with Celia, who was equally incensed.

"Unless there's something else that you'd like to say or show me, I think we're done here," Charlize said.

Celia shook her head. Charlize stood up and extended her hand toward Celia.

"Thank you very much for your time today, and I wish you all the best."

Celia stared at the hand for a few moments, resisting the urge to slap it away. She decided to take the higher road and shook it.

"Thank you for having me. I hope that sometime in the near future you will come around because I'm sure some of your clients will want to use our products."

Charlize smiled.

"We'll cross that bridge when we get there. However, if I were you, I wouldn't count on it too much," Charlize replied. She sauntered away, heading up the stairs to the mezzanine floor office.

"What the hell was that?" Celia asked, fuming.

"Trust me, I'm just as angry as you are. You warned me about how difficult she might be. I didn't know it would be this bad," Melanie replied.

"Hadn't you briefed her?"

"Of course, I had. I didn't set you up. I honestly thought we had smoothed things over, but she was clearly holding another ace up her sleeve," Melanie replied.

"I have met disrespectful people, but this was a stab in the back and one the worst interactions I have ever had!" Celia said. "I think you should reconsider this business partnership. It won't end well."

"Let me straighten this out. I'm not taking any more of this. I'm really sorry that it turned out like this."

"I'm sorry too," Celia replied as they both stood up.

Celia packed the beauty products she had laid out on the table.

Minutes later, she was ready to leave. She looked up to the mezzanine floor where the upper office was. Through its windows, she could see Melanie and

Charlize having an intense argument. She couldn't hear what they were saying.

'That soundproofing must have cost a good amount,' Celia thought to herself as she walked out. It felt good to feel the afternoon sun again after the cold reception she had received. She needed to see her sons. They were the perfect antidote to the negative emotions she was dealing with.

"What do you mean, red in color? You know the boy doesn't like red."

Celia had just walked into an intense conversation between her mother and Mrs. Owens on speakerphone.

"Oh, but he is only turning nine years old! He can learn about new colors, you know! Also, how about throwing in a clown or two?" Mrs. Owen's voice crackled through the speakerphone.

"He's turning eight, Christie. You want to bring a clown? Have you seen James? He has never and will never like clowns," Audrey replied animatedly.

"Audrey, you need to open your mind to new things!" Mrs. Owens replied.

"No, Christie. We don't do red colored things or clowns here. Even Christmas is just a regular day with a touch of smart clothes. No red in sight."

Celia listened, with her smile growing ever wider. She waved at her mother, who waved back and pointed towards the phone, shrugging her shoulders in wonderment at Mrs. Owens strange ideas.

"Maybe I should come over and we can talk better face-to-face?" Mrs. Owens suggested.
"No! Not now, Christie! The boys will be arriving soon from the school trip and I don't want them bogged down by our chat about this."

"It will only take a minute, Audrey."

"Tomorrow. Does tomorrow work for you?"

Mrs. Owens sighed. "Very well. Tomorrow morning it is."

"Perfect. They won't be around to hear our plans.

A horn sounded from outside. The boys had arrived.

"I have to go now, Christie. Enjoy your evening."

"Sure, and remember..." She didn't finish as Audrey had already hung up and was walking swiftly to the door.

"These guys are right on time!" Audrey said as she

opened the door.

The boys barged in with their little travel packs, still buzzing with excitement.

"And then, and then we saw lions." James shouted.

"You saw a lion? Were you scared?" Audrey asked.

"No! The lion was locked in a cage!" he replied.

Audrey gave Celia a look.

"We have to change that image. You know lions aren't meant to be in cages," Audrey said as she led them to their bedrooms.

Alone now, Celia slumped onto the couch and it wasn't long before she drifted off into a deep sleep.

She was startled awake by a noise. She could hear the shrieks and laughter of the kids filtering in from the backyard garden. She couldn't believe they were still playing after such a long day trip.

She looked at the clock. It was five o'clock in the evening. The noise was still there. A buzzing sound. It was her phone, which was inside her handbag. She quickly searched for it and took it out. It was Melanie. Celia cleared her throat.

"Hello, Mel," she said.

"Where are you?" Melanie said.

"I am not coming if she wants to have another chat," she replied.

There was a brief pause. She could hear sniffling sounds.

"Are you okay, Mel?" Celia asked.

"Not quite. We won't be smoothing things over anytime soon, actually."

"She's that stubborn, huh?"

"Not that. Can you come over, please? Now?"

"What's going on, Mel?"

"Please come over. I need you, Cece."

"Can you tell me what's going on?" Celia asked as she grabbed her bag, put on her shoes and walked towards the door.

"Charlize is… she's lying on the floor. She's not moving. I think she's dead and I don't know what to do," a distraught Melanie managed to say over the phone.

Her words struck Celia like a thunderbolt.

5

Celia got to the nail parlor in less than thirty minutes.

Outside, the flashing emergency lights from an ambulance were lighting up the street. A small crowd was gathering outside as curious people wondered what was going on. Celia ran into the building and found Melanie confused.

"What happened?" Celia asked as her eyes took in the scene.

In front of them, at the foot of the staircase that led to the mezzanine office, were two paramedics. Charlize's dead body lay in between them at the bottom of a staircase from the mezzanine floor. They were not conducting any emergency procedures, which was not a good sign. Celia looked around and saw the two parlor employees, Sarah and Fidel, who were in shock. What had they witnessed? she wondered.

Melanie was quietly sobbing, her hands clasped together as if in prayer for a miracle. However, Celia knew better, there was no way Charlize was rising again.

"Mel, you want to tell me what happened?"

Melanie nodded as she worked to compose herself.

"We were talking. Stuff about the business. Then she walked out and the next thing I know she was tumbling down the stairs."

"You saw her tumbling down?" the detective asked.

"I heard it first. It was like a rumble. At first, I thought the mezzanine floor was collapsing, so I ran out for dear life. Then at the top of the stairs I caught her taking the last few steps to the bottom." She paused. "I... I tried calling out to her. She wasn't moving. She wasn't breathing. I ran down and... I can't believe this is happening."

Celia massaged her back to comfort her friend, but it sounded to her like this was an accident. She could see both Charlize's heels were off, lying a short distance from her body. Had she tripped on one, missed a step?

She looked again at Fidel and Sarah, who were silently conversing. Maybe they saw more that could explain the situation.

"Let me ask your people," Celia said.

She was about to move towards the two employees when the police walked in. Two plain-clothes detectives followed two uniformed officers as they strode straight to where Charlize lay. Talking to the employees would have to wait, Celia resolved.

After conversing with the paramedics, the two detectives walked to where Melanie and Celia stood. The tall and hulky one took out a notebook and spoke while the slender one scanned the room.

"You're the lady who called?" the detective asked.

Melanie nodded.

"Your name, please, and your connection to the deceased?"

"Melanie Dawes. We're business partners," she replied. He quickly scribbled her responses.
The detective then asked for the identities of Celia and the two employees, which he also wrote down.

"Alright, tell me what happened here," the detective asked.

Melanie took in a deep breath then told him the

same thing she had recounted to Celia.

"What were you talking about before the incident?" the detective queried.

"It was about a business deal that she wanted to make."

"What was the nature of the conversation?"

"What do you mean?"

"Was it cordial or more heated?"

Melanie hesitated, then responded. "It was more of an argument."

The detective's eyes narrowed. Then he wrote this detail down. Celia's eyes widened. Why had Melanie left out this detail earlier?

The paramedics had already left, and three forensic investigators had replaced them. They were taking pictures, samples, and looking for clues on the staircase as well as the mezzanine office.

"So, tell me again, why were you arguing?" the detective probed.

"It was something that happened often. You know, it's the norm in a business relationship," Melanie replied.

Celia wanted to pinch her now, because her responses did not sound very convincing.

"I know many business relationships where people don't argue much. Would you say you got along?"

"For the most part, yes."

"And for the other part?"

"It was…"

Melanie trailed off as she turned to look at Celia. Celia maintained a deadpan expression. She didn't want the detective knowing she was pinching her friend to keep quiet.

After a pause, the slender detective returned and whispered to the tall one. Celia would have wanted to do the same, but she feared that if the detectives saw any sign of scheming behavior, they might see Melanie in an unfavorable light.

It was too late, though.

The tall detective returned, handcuffs in hand.

"I'm going to take you into custody now, Miss Dawes," he said as he reached for her hands.

"Wait, what for?"

"You're under suspicion for the death of the deceased," he replied, locking both cuffs around her wrists.

Celia couldn't believe her eyes.

As they walked out into the street, the small crowd had grown larger. They saw Melanie being marched out, and it hit Celia what a spectacle it was.

"Don't let them take me," Melanie said to Celia. "I didn't do anything."

"I know. I'm right behind you," Celia replied.

Melanie gave Celia one forlorn look as she was led to the police car. For Celia, the whole ordeal was surreal.

Celia quickly went into the parlor and told the two employees to monitor the place and the investigators until she got back. She then dashed to her car just as the police car sped off. As she fumbled to get her car keys out and start the engine, adrenaline was pumping fast in her system.

She followed them all the way to the station. While driving she kept trying to come to terms with the image of her good friend handcuffed and led out in

public like a guilty criminal. It wasn't adding up. Maybe it was an accident. On the other hand, it was simply a case of being at the wrong place at the wrong time. But even Celia had to admit it didn't look good for Melanie. For now, all she could do to prevent the helplessness from paralyzing her was to show her support.
When they got to the station, Melanie was swiftly booked in and then led down the corridor to the interrogation room.

Celia waited in the lobby alone, seated on the wooden bench that had seen better days. She reached for her phone and dialed a familiar number.

"Hey Cece, what's up?" Chloe asked on the other end of the line.

"Hey. Something's happened. Melanie has been arrested," Celia said.

"Wait, what?" Chloe asked in shock.

"Yeah. I'm at the station now, waiting to see what happens."

 "How on Earth did that happen?"

Celia sighed, wondering whether to reveal the weight of the news.

"Something tragic happened at the nail parlor. Do you have a moment to come over?" she asked.

"Yeah sure, I'll be leaving in half an hour."

"Great. See you soon," she replied.

She lowered her phone, then stared at its screen.

"Is this the part where you call me?" A voice asked.

She looked up to find detective Bill Koloane staring down at her. Even in these testing times, she still found him disarmingly attractive. He was dressed sharply as usual with khaki pants, a striped long-sleeve shirt and brown shoes. His scalp shone under the glare of the house lights, and his beard had grown fuller.

She tried to smile back but didn't succeed.

"I don't think I'll need to do that now that you're here," she replied.

"Are you okay?" he asked.

"I'm not actually. You remember Melanie Dawes?"

"She works at the library, right?"

"Yes. Well, I'm here because she's been arrested for

something she might not have done."

Detective Koloane sat down next to her. "How serious is this?" he asked.

"Her business partner fell down a flight of stairs and the police suspect that Melanie did it."

"Any special reason?"

"They had a heated argument before her fall. Melanie witnessed her fall."

"Hmm," Detective Koloane grunted, "That's serious."

"I am just trying to wrap my head around what happened."

"Was this a business dispute?" he asked.

Celia turned to him, wondering why he was asking her that question.

"Are you on the case?" she asked.

"I'm not at the moment. It hasn't been assigned to me. I have no idea what they're doing with her in the interrogation room."

"Then I hope you understand if I can't answer your question at the moment because I'm not sure it was."

"Fair enough," he replied. "Anything you want me to do to help?"

"Just go and check for me that she's okay and advise me on whether I should stay or do something else."

"Sure thing."

With that, Bill Koloane got up, walked down the hall towards the interrogation room, and disappeared around the corner.

One hour later, he returned. By that time, Chloe had arrived and was keeping Celia company.

"I'm being informed that after answering some questions, Melanie has decided to ask for a lawyer. So, she's going to the holding cell for the rest of the day until her lawyer comes over," he said.

"Has she made the phone call to the lawyer?" Chloe asked.

"I'm told that that has been done now though I do not know when he's going to come over. I would suggest that you leave, and I'll keep you posted on how things are going."

"Can I see her?" Celia prodded.

"Unfortunately, no. It's not allowed."

Celia thought for a moment. She turned to Chloe.

"I think one of us needs to stay here just in case something comes up. The other one needs to go and check on the nail parlor."

"I can keep watch over here. Run to the parlor and stay safe," Chloe said.

"Stay safe, too," Celia said.

"I'm at the police station. I'll be fine," Chloe said with a smile.

Then Celia remembered that Chloe was the daughter of one of the richest men in town. She wasn't going to be touched by anyone.

Celia stood up.

"Thanks for the help," Celia said as she turned to look at Bill. "Chloe will keep tabs on things."

Celia drove back to the nail parlor as promised. She found Fidel still there as forensic Detectives kept looking for clues around the staircase and the mezzanine office. Charlize's body had been taken away, leaving behind chalk marks to show where she had been found.

"They tell me they are just finishing up," Fidel said.

Celia nodded her head as she watched them finalize their investigation of the scene. They rolled out a fresh length of crime scene tape that blocked off the section leading to the staircase. She knew that she wouldn't be accessing that place anytime soon.

As the investigators left, one of them stopped to talk to Celia and Fidel.

"I would suggest that you don't touch anything around that area for the next forty-eight hours. We will know if you manipulated this place. Sorry for your loss."

Celia and Fidel exchanged looks after the detectives left.

"Hello, is everything ok?"

Celia turned to find Patricia Nesbitt standing at the entrance of the nail parlor.

"Can I help you?" Celia asked.

"I'm actually wondering if I can help you," Patricia replied.

"We are handling things, thank you," Celia replied, keen to make her leave.

"I'm not here to be a bother, and I'm actually the fellow business just down the street. I'm just here to show my support. Sorry for the loss of Charlize."

Celia nodded her head slowly.

"Life is short, isn't it?" Patricia said.

"Yes, it is."

"I mean, one minute you're gloating about running me and my business out of town and the next, you're lying dead on the floor. Such a pity."

Although she wasn't smiling as she said this, Patricia's words weren't exactly a show of sympathy.

"I'm going to ask you to leave now. Thank you for passing by," Celia said.

"Sorry to intrude, but I couldn't help coming. I'll be on my way."

Patricia turned to walk away and caught herself at the last moment.

"Just one more thing. I think we'll be seeing more of each other in the coming days. Just as a show of support," Patricia said with a wry smile.

She sauntered away with a spring in her step,

confirming Celia's suspicions. This was definitely someone who had something to gain from the death of Charlize.

6

The next day, after she was done with her client visits in the morning, Celia went to check on Melanie at the station.

She had brought with her some muffins that her mother had baked, hoping that she'd be allowed to give them to Melanie. She was searched to ensure she didn't have any weapons. She had to leave her keys and other metallic objects in a safe. Surprisingly, the pack of muffins wasn't barred.

"Yes, you can see her," the officer at the desk said, much to Celia's relief.

She was taken to a visitors' room, where she waited. It was a drab place with grey concrete walls everywhere. A heavily grilled window was open.

Melanie walked in looking a little ruffled, but at least she had a smile on her face.

"It's so good to see you," Melanie said as she took a seat. A policeman stood at the door, watching them.

"How was your night?" Celia asked.

"I didn't sleep much. But I survived," Melanie replied.

"Chloe was here till yesterday evening, if it helps. We're here for you."

"For Chloe to stay that long, then I feel blessed. Thank you."

"I got you some muffins," Celia said as she passed the small pack to her.

"Hey, no. You can't do that here!" The policeman shouted as he marched toward them.

"Okay, sorry. I'll just take them back," Celia said as she reached for the pack.

"No, I'll take them now. Have to check," the policeman said as he grabbed the pack. "Continue"

He moved back to the door.

"I hope he won't have eaten them by the time we are done," Celia said.

"I could have done with one of those! It was lukewarm tea and dry bread this morning. A fitting way to remember yesterday's interrogation."

"Did they question you for a long time?"

"When alone, it was short. Then I could remember you pinching me and I knew I shouldn't talk too much. I called my lawyer."

"Did they show up?"

"Yes. Later in the day. Then we did another session and my lawyer did most of the talking. I could tell they were a little frustrated," Melanie replied.

"Meaning they believe you did it."

"I may have been at the top of the staircase during the last moments of her fall, but I didn't cause it. But it's very hard to prove that without CCTV footage," Melanie replied.

"What do you mean? The cameras weren't working?"

"The cameras don't cover the top of the staircase, so you can't tell. You just see her tumbling," Melanie replied.

"We'll need to get that checked as soon as you get

out."

Melanie shook her head, then buried her face in her hands for a moment. When she lifted her face back up, it was as if she had seen something.

"As hard as it is to say, I think either Charlize tripped, was unwell or... Or threw herself down the stairs," Melanie said.

"Threw herself? No, she didn't look like the type to do that," Celia said.

"But what other explanation is there?"

"There must be one. However, the suicide theory is outrageous," Celia replied firmly.

"Then help me solve this," Melanie said, reaching for Celia's hand, "Talk to Fidel and Sarah for me. I know they've talked to the cops. Find out if they saw something that could set me free."

Celia pondered this for a moment.

"Okay, I'll do that. Let's see what they have to say."

Later that day, Celia managed to call Sarah and Fidel to a meeting.

She had toyed around with the idea of meeting them

at a restaurant for a more relaxed atmosphere, but she opted not to. She figured that it made more sense to talk to them together at the location where the tragedy happened.

Maybe the emotional gravity of the situation would clear their heads about what they saw at the time. It even gave the opportunity for them to walk through Charlize's last moments, a benefit of being right at the location. This way, she could spot any inaccuracies or blind spots in their stories.

She found them waiting for her at the entrance. She had taken the key from Fidel so neither employee could get in.

"Sorry to keep you waiting, guys," she said, opening the door.

Celia ushered them in and led them to the waiting couch. They sat next to each other with a pillow's width between them. She pulled a chair and sat facing them.

"As you both know, I'm Melanie's good friend, Celia. The last couple of days have not been easy for any of us I'm sure. Especially for you. You lost one of your bosses and it's not easy finding a new job in this town," she said as she cast an eye towards Fidel.

"It will be resolved somehow," Sarah said.

"That's exactly why I'm here. I'm curious to find out what happened. So, feel free to share what you saw. We can start with you, Sarah. What did you see?"

 Sarah took a deep breath.

"I was busy with a client at the time. I was fully focused on doing her toenails. So obviously, my whole attention was towards the floor. For some reason I turned around toward the steps, and that's the same time when I heard..." Sarah paused at this moment, as if she was remembering the trauma of what happened, "...when I heard her falling down the stairs."

"What happened after that?" Celia asked.

"Everything was crazy. By the time I figured out what was happening, Fidel was already next to her, checking her pulse and... and then he confirmed that she was gone."

"Who called for an ambulance?"

"Melanie did," Sarah replied.

 Celia turned to Fidel, who was fiddling with his fingers as he listened to Sarah speak.

"Fidel, what happened?" Celia asked.

"I was with a client as well, just like Sarah. We were chatting a lot. You know, keeping her busy because that's what I do when clients come over. I keep them busy and happy with stories. I was also distracted just like Sarah and I didn't see what happened before Charlize fell down the stairs."

"But you responded faster than Sarah," Celia said.

"I guess I've got good reflexes," he replied.

Celia was not convinced.

"Were you in the army or special forces or something?" she asked.

Fidel shook his head.

"No, I've seen a lot of things in the street. When you grow up in a dangerous neighborhood, you grow up more alert than many people do."

"Fidel your reflexes were fantastic. I'm amazed that you were able to get there as soon as Charlize landed at the bottom of the stairs. Is there something else you might have heard or seen just before she fell?"

Sarah and Fidel exchanged looks. Fidel turned to Celia, shaking his head.

"I wish I could say more but that's all I know."

"Since you were at the foot of the stairs first, where was Melanie at that time" Celia probed.

"She was standing at the top of the stairs, looking down on us," he replied.

"What was her face like?"

"She looked shocked. It's not something she expected, I guess," he said.

Celia was interrupted by a loud knock on the door. She looked up, puzzled. She wasn't able to see who it was because of the stickers on the window front. She just hoped it wasn't Patricia Nesbitt again.

"Any of you expecting someone?" Celia asked.

Fidel shook his head, and Sarah shrugged.

Celia arose and walked to the door. When she opened it, a tall graceful woman in sunglasses walked in. She stopped at the center of the room, looking around at the ceiling and the fittings and everything in between not saying a word.

"Excuse me, can I help you?" Celia asked.

The woman took off her sunglasses and smiled.

"I'm looking for Melanie Dawes," the woman said in

a sultry, authoritative voice.

 "She's not here at the moment. Who's asking?"

"My name is Gloria Langa, sister to the late Charlize Langa. And you are?"

"Celia Dube, a friend of Melanie's. Did you just say you are Charlize's sister?"

"Half-sister actually. We share the same father," Gloria replied.

"Sorry for your loss," Celia said.

"It shall be well, as they say. How do I find Melanie?"

 Celia wondered whether to respond to her or just let it slide.

"She's with the police currently helping them with their investigation," she replied.

"I see. Well, here's my card. I would really like to talk to her. The moment you see her, kindly let her know. My family is very interested in the various pursuits she was involved in," Gloria said.

"Sure thing. I'll do that."

Gloria Langa smiled, put on her sunglasses, and cat

walked away.

Celia turned to the two workers.

"Any of you saw her before?"

Neither employee had ever seen her. This thing was turning into a maze with hidden trap doors that she could fall through at any moment.

7

Having gotten nowhere the previous day, Celia decided to change her approach with the employees. She met them both for breakfast at the Pier, each an hour apart. She talked to Sarah first as she had her coffee and pancakes covered in maple syrup. It made her a little more forthcoming with information.

"Charlize was smart. Brilliant. She had an answer to everything," Sarah said in between mouthfuls.

"She was good with the clients too?" Celia asked.

"Yes, she was. She was very courteous and knew how to handle their issues. She added little perks, like giving them coffee or wine or even candy. She's the one who really taught us a new way of handling clients," Sarah replied.

"Was she strict?"

"Always. She kept time, always the first one to arrive

and the last to leave. She made us keep track of all transactions. Our breaks were timed to the last second. She was a military sergeant, to be honest."

"What about her other side? Did she ever get angry?"

"Oh, yes. She had a short fuse. I think all perfectionists are like that. Very good at what they do, but if you fall short, they're like sharks. They can tear you to pieces," Sarah said.

"So, did she tear you to pieces often?"

"That usually happened if you really messed up. I think she gave me a talking to around thrice. It wasn't a pleasant experience. She made you feel small. If my mother had not taught me how to deal with negative comments, I'd be depressed right now," she said.

"I see," Celia said. If Charlize had flown off the lid and Melanie felt slighted, might she have acted in the spur of the moment, resulting in the tragic accident?

Celia caught herself. She couldn't believe that she was even thinking her friend might be guilty of something so hideous.

"After sleeping on it, do you remember something new about what happened that day?" Celia asked.

Sarah paused for a moment, her chin working as she enjoyed the last bite of her pancake.

"No, I'm sorry. It's the same recollection as yesterday. I wish I had more to say," she replied.

Twenty minutes later, Fidel sat in front of Celia. He was having porridge with a cob of boiled corn. A great meal that would keep you running for most of the day without hunger pangs. He was hungry and ate the meal ravenously. She let him finish first before they talked.

"You had a great night?" Celia asked.

He nodded.

"Yes. It was good. Short but good," he replied.

"Do you have a family?"

"They are not here. They live in the village. I wouldn't be able to afford to have them over."

"It makes sense. So, did you get to think afresh about what happened to Charlize?"

He shook his head.

"No, nothing new came to mind."

"Are you sure? Considering you attended to her

pretty quickly. Maybe…"

"It doesn't change anything. I didn't see anything that could help," he replied.

Celia got the sense he didn't want to talk about it.

"Is this uncomfortable for you?"

"What?" he asked.

"Does talking about the event make you uncomfortable?" she asked again.

"Isn't talking about someone's death supposed to be? It's a hard thing. I'm not sure if I'll be fired tomorrow because of this," he replied.

Celia was surprised by this. She hadn't seen it that way. If he knew something, why would he incriminate his remaining boss?

"I understand. She's my friend too, you know. I'm just trying to help," Celia replied.
Fidel stared outside for a moment, then turned back to her.

"Sometimes, it's better to let things fix themselves. The universe won't fail her," he said.

Celia didn't understand him. There was a wall there. She had to find another way of reaching out to him.

During lunch hour, Celia was checking the equipment after the staff had left for their break when she heard the door open. A sharply dressed, clean-shaven man carrying a briefcase walked towards her.

"Hello there. I'm looking for Melanie Dawes?"

Celia braced herself. This trend of strangers looking for Melanie was worrying. She knew this was going to be another surprise.

"She's not here, Can I help you?"

"My name is Michael Nzomo. I'm Charlize Langa's lawyer. I'm here to discuss Charlize's will?"

Celia's antennas went up.

"What about her will?" she asked.

Michael handed her a piece of paper.

"According to her will, all the shares that she had in this business automatically come under my guardianship as her lawyer. Any proceeds of a sale, if it happens, will go to the family."

"Oh, wow," Celia said as she read the document. It

was an official notice that simply stated his newfound status in the nail parlor.

"So, I wanted to come around and see what I'll be working with. I trust that you are going to be open tomorrow?"

"Yes, we shall be open tomorrow," Celia replied.

"Fantastic. Kindly inform Melanie that I'll be passing by."

As abruptly as he had come, Michael left.

Celia needed to see Melanie.

*

"It's starting to feel like you want to be in here with me," Melanie said with a smile.

"Why do you say that?" Celia asked.

"You have visited me every single day. That's impressive," she replied.

"Well, there's always something new in this story. I'm starting to feel like I'm walking through a maze," Celia replied.

"What did Sarah and Fidel tell you yesterday?"

"Nothing much. Neither of them saw anything before Charlize fell down the stairs."

Melanie shook her head.

"Fidel knows something. He may not be willing to talk, but I saw it in his eyes when he looked at me," Melanie said.

"Are you serious? What do you mean?" Celia probed.

"After Charlize fell, I was standing at the top of the stairs. He looked at me with the kind of look that said he saw something. At the time, I felt like he understood that I was not responsible for it. But now it feels like he's holding back for some reason," she explained.

"I see. But a look doesn't say much you know," Celia said.

"You need to do your thing, Celia. You're good at making people talk."

"I think you're overestimating my powers, Melanie."

"I know what I'm talking about. Remember, we solved the case together last time."

"I'm not promising you anything, but I'll see what I can do," she said.

Celia took out the letter from the lawyer and placed it in front of Melanie.

"Charlize's lawyer came by and left this."

Without responding, Melanie read the letter. Her rising eyebrows told Celia she was surprised by its contents.

"This is new. So, is he going to be coming to the parlor every day?" she asked.

"I don't know. However, he's coming in tomorrow. He's hoping to see you, actually.

Speaking of which, you should be out of here already. Forty-eight hours have passed. Have they set a date for a bail hearing or are they planning to release you?" Celia asked.

Melanie shook her head.

"I think you're overestimating the amount of luck I'm having right now. I'm not getting out, Cece," Melanie said.

"What are you talking about?"

"They've found some new evidence. Charlize had poison in her system when she died. It could have been administered by anyone two hours before she fell down the stairs," Melanie said matter-of-factly.

Celia was taken aback.

"If it was just a fall down the stairs, I was facing manslaughter. I'm looking at a murder charge now." Melanie said, breaking down in tears.

8

Celia woke up to high-pitched voices filtering into her bedroom.

At first, she thought it was part of a dream. But the more she strained her ears, the clearer the voices became.

"You have no clue why I am choosing purple. It is the color of nobility, luxury, power, and creativity. It's a good thing for the boy to make wishes with such a great theme color."

"But these are two boys! They need active intense colors like red and screaming orange!"

"The only screaming we need is that of joy from the boys, not the one you are doing right now."

"That's an insult now, Audrey. I didn't come all the way here to be insulted."

Celia tried to cover her head with a pillow, but it didn't help. She had hardly slept the night before, filling out transaction reports for the sales she had done that week. She then dropped the boys off at school and drove back home to sneak in a quick nap before starting her day. Now that she had been woken by the argument between her mother and Mrs. Owens, there was no way she was going back to sleep.

When she walked into the living room, she found the two women seated opposite each other, in silent resignation.

"It's too beautiful a morning to be arguing" Celia said.

"Who said we were arguing?" Audrey asked.

"Ma, you woke me up from my nap. Now I have to endure sleepwalking for the rest of the day," she replied.

"Cece, you should weigh in on this. What color should we use for the theme party, red or purple?" Mrs. Owens asked.

"She doesn't need to vote," Audrey chimed in.

"But since we can't agree she can break the stalemate," Mrs. Owens insisted.

"No ladies, I will not be that person. I think this is a good time for you to find a way to meet halfway. You've been friends for too long not to figure this out," Celia replied.

"You're just going to leave us in limbo?" Mrs. Owens asked.

"It's only limbo if you let it," Celia replied as she turned toward the kitchen. "Oh, and you have till evening to agree. Otherwise I'll take over the planning."

*

The Police Station was busy that day. Celia counted fifteen criminals brought in within a half-hour period, the highest she had witnessed that week. There must be a crackdown of some sort, she thought.

She was seated on the old bench once again, waiting. The police station hallway had become all-too familiar by now. The noise of protesting suspects, phones ringing and chatter by detectives, slamming office and cell doors and footsteps all colored Celia's wait for Melanie to be released on bail.

The situation felt too real, almost as if it was Celia herself facing trial. If this was happening to her, it might have torn her to pieces because she would spend all of her time worrying about her boys.

She saw Detective Bill Koloane walking down the hallway with another detective, having a conversation. Impatient, she stood up and walked to him.

"Excuse me, detective," she said.

Bill turned to her and smiled.

"You're here for Melanie?" he asked.

"Yes. I'm hoping she's coming out soon?"

"They're just processing her. She should be out in about five minutes," he replied.

Bill waved off his fellow detective so he could spend some time with Celia.

"How are you holding up?" he asked.

"This whole thing is a bit unusual for me. I've never

been to the police station this many times. I don't know what to say," she replied.

"There's no getting used to this kind of thing," he said.

"Do you like the gray walls that you see every day?" she asked.

"I enjoy imagining the number of colors I want to paint on them every day," he said.

They both laughed.

"Is that your version of hope?" she asked.

"Something like that," Bill replied.

Just then, Melanie came walking towards them, followed by a police officer. She was dressed in a fresh pair of clothes that Celia had brought for her previously. She still looked a little disheveled, but it was a blessing to Celia for her to see her friend walking freely again.

"I'll leave you guys," Bill said with a smile as he walked away.

Melanie and Celia embraced tightly.

"Thank you for coming to get me," Melanie said.

"That's what sisters are for. Come on, let's get out of here."

"Right now, I'm craving one thing: some chicken biryani."

"I'm sure we can take a detour on our way home."

"Let's not go home. After we get something to eat, I'd like to see the nail parlor," Melanie replied.

"Are you sure about that?"

"Positive."

After a hearty meal of chicken biryani, which was full of great rice and spicy chicken, they got to the nail parlor. Melanie walked around as if she was in a daze.

It looked like she was reliving everything that happened the day Charlize died. Celia was unsure whether to interrupt her or to let her deal with the memory.

"Are you okay, Mel?" she finally asked.

Melanie nodded and continued her walk around the space.

"Excuse me, is anybody home?"

Celia turned towards the door and saw Patricia already standing in the space. Melanie seemed to be oblivious to the new entrant. Celia walked up to Patricia.

"I thought we had an agreement that you wouldn't be coming here on short notice?" Celia said in a low tone.

"I saw Melanie coming in and I just had to come in and check on her," Patricia replied.

"She's fine, as you can see. Can you leave now?" Celia said, firmly.

"I actually wanted to talk to her because I had a proposition for her," Patricia said.
"I'm telling you that this is not the time to have that conversation. So, can you leave, please?"

"What conversation?" Melanie asked. Celia turned to find Melanie already standing next to her.

"Hello Melanie. I'm so sorry to hear what happened. I hope that this whole situation is resolved so that we can have you back on Main Street doing what you love," Patricia said.

Celia wished she could wipe the smirk off her mouth.

"Thank you for your kind words, Patricia. What's on

your mind?" Melanie replied.

"Well, the main reason I'd like to have you back on the Main Street is so that we can have a very healthy conversation about your nail parlor. I'd be interested to buy it if it's on the market," Patricia explained.

"If it's on the market now? Why would it be on the market?"

"A nail parlor is not easy to run. Ask me, I've been doing this for eight years. I wouldn't want this fantastic establishment to just go to waste because of some challenges."

"What are you trying to say, Patricia?"

"Well, it's no secret that you're facing some legal challenges right now and so you're not able to run the business. Let me take it out of your hands so it you can focus on what's important and get your life back together," she added.

Melanie's eyes grew red with rage. Celia knew she was about to implode.

"I think this is your time to leave now, Patricia," Celia said as she gently pushed Patricia towards the door.

"At least tell me you'll give it some thought. I know time is not exactly on our side, but..."

Celia didn't let her finish. She ushered Patricia gently out, then closed the door and locked it.

"I'm sorry about that," Celia said.

"Has she been here while I was away?" Melanie asked.

"Yes, she has. Once. But I drove her out," she replied.

"They are hunting me down, Cece. And I don't know if I have the strength to keep running. You have to help me fix this," Melanie said, running her hand through her hair.

And at that moment Celia realized that she was possibly the only person who believed Melanie was innocent. But if Melanie didn't do it, then who did?

9

It was clear to see that Patricia's visit had triggered something on the inside of Melanie that she had been trying to suppress for the past few days.

Patricia had the kind of personality that was very hard to trust. She reminded Celia of those street moneychangers who dazzle you with their cards and take flight after making you lose all your hard-earned cash.

"I think we should just keep an eye on her and see what else she has up her sleeve. Right?" Celia said.

"Definitely. Now that I'm here, I'm feeling a heaviness about having it open," Melanie said.

"What's going through your mind?" Celia asked.

Melanie sighed.

"I'm not comfortable staying open until after

Charlize's funeral."

"But I think this is what Charlize would have wanted. To keep the dream alive," she replied.

"I just feel it's disrespectful. Closing would be like flying the flag at half mast," she said.

"Sounds like giving up on the dream. You know how you can make it worthwhile? Put up a desk with photos of her and a condolence book. It would honor her memory," Celia said.

Melanie pondered this for a moment, then nodded.

"You're right. I like that. We can pay tribute to her," she replied.

"It will also be good for the clients who knew her," she added.

"I really need to find out what happened to her. Where was she poisoned? How did that happen?"

"I'm with you on that. Something sinister happened. The threat might be closer than it seems," Celia replied.

"What do you think we should do?"

"We should start with the guest list during your

launch. It's possible that the person who did it was part of that event," Celia said.

"Got some time to help me with that?" Melanie asked.

Celia glanced at her wristwatch.

"No, I have an appointment with a client in an hour. I have to head out now. How about coffee later? Chloe wants to see you too," she said.

"Sure, we can do coffee," Melanie mumbled.

Celia smiled, then left.

*

Later that day, the three friends, Melanie, Celia and Chloe, congregated at a local cafe.

"It's so great to see you out and free Mel," Chloe said.

"It's great. Although I feel like I constantly have to watch my back because I don't know who might come for me next," Melanie said.

"Who'll come for you next?" Chloe asked.

"The police. The person who did it. Who knows?" Melanie replied.

"Your recent experience has made you more cautious. Don't let it get to you, Mel. You'll get through this. Keep your head up," Celia said.

"That's easier said than done. Think about it this way: I have no witnesses or evidence to prove my innocence. The CCTV footage at the top of the stairs has a blind spot. How do I defend myself?"

"You have us Melanie, we're here for you," Chloe said.

"She's got a point there, though. The evidence is stacked up against her and I think it'll be a problem to make her case. You've got a great lawyer in Collins Rebbe," Celia said.

"Should I look for a proper criminal lawyer, though? This type of crime isn't his speciality," Melanie said.

"Don't change your lawyer. Stick with him for these two reasons: he's a great lawyer, and we'll help you find the evidence you need," Celia said.

"I agree with Cece. Collins has been great for us, even with some serious lawsuits that would have brought down our company. He'll raise his game," Chloe said.

"Alright. I'll keep my fingers crossed," Melanie said.

"Guys, why are we talking about depressing stuff? We should light up the place a bit," Chloe said, "How about we do that blind date?"

Melanie and Celia looked at each other.

"It'll be fine, Cece. It's just an evening out. Plus, if it doesn't work out, we can always call it an evening earlier than planned. You're game?" Chloe asked.

"Alright fine. There's no point of fighting it anymore. When do you plan to do it?" Celia asked.

"About this weekend on Saturday evening?" Chloe asked.

"Works for me," Melanie said.

"I'll make arrangements to have my mum watch the kids," Celia replied.

"Great! I'll keep you posted on developments," Chloe

said.

"One more thing, Chloe. Your family is connected in certain places. What do you know about the Langa family?"

"You're talking about Frasier Langa, the real estate and timber magnate?"

"I'm not sure. His daughter is Gloria Langa."

"Yes, he's the one. He's got many children from several wives. It's an interesting situation, but he has the money to handle them, I guess. He's been part of quite a number of government deals too. Why?"

"Just curious. We happen to know one of his daughters. She's, as you say, quite interesting," Celia remarked.

"Has she done something crazy?"

"No, nothing. At least not yet."

"Alright. Sorry I don't know much more about them," Chloe said.

"I think we've got more than enough information to know who we're dealing with," Celia said.

It was late evening when Celia and Melanie got back

to the nail parlor. They found Fidel and Sarah cleaning the place before they left for the day. Celia found it refreshing that the staff were managing through the difficult circumstances. It was a good sign that the business would bounce back.

Melanie was about to go up the stairs when a man came in. He was a very muscular man in a dark suit. He walked with a confident, agile gait. He had a neck tattoo that peeked from his shirt collar.

He didn't say a word. He simply walked straight up to Melanie as if he knew her. Melanie didn't flinch. He handed her a white envelope, then swiftly turned and walked out. Celia was intrigued.

"Who on earth was that?" Celia asked.

"No one you should know," Melanie said.

"Don't play games now. Who was that?" Celia insisted.

By this time, Melanie was already reading the letter. The more she read, the more her expression became grave. When she was done, she folded the letter.

"I'm waiting," Celia said.

"We took a loan for the business. Charlize made the deal. Now, the lenders want their money back,"

Melanie said.

"Who are these people you borrowed money from? Because that doesn't look like someone you should be making deals with," she said.

"It's a loan shark," she whispered.

"You took money from a loan shark? On a business that's hardly started building a client base?" Celia exclaimed.

"It was pretty stupid now that I think about it. Anyway, that's water under the bridge. I have forty-eight hours to come up with the money and I don't know how that's going to happen."

"So, what are you going to do?" she asked.

"I'm going to have to find it somehow or they might put a gun to my head," she replied.

10

"Have you made up your minds about this?" Celia asked.

She stood at the end of the kitchen table, eating the last piece of buttermilk rusk, a tasty dry biscuit that she usually had with her morning coffee.

"Well, we're supposed to talk about it today," Audrey replied.

"But we agreed that if there was no progress by now, I would take over. Right? "Celia asked.

"That's true but…"

"No buts, Ma," Celia said.

Audrey stopped stirring the pot of tomato soup that she was making.

"You should understand that we're simply two passionate people working on this. So it will take us some time," Audrey said.

"Time's not on my side, Ma. We need to shop, send invites, decide on work to be done. If we want other kids to attend the party, we need to give their parents enough notice, don't you think?"

"We'll make the decision today, I promise."

"No Ma. I'll move ahead with the plan I have in mind."

"And what plan is that?" Audrey queried.

"You'll see it unfold very soon," Celia replied with a cheeky grin.

*

It was strange to walk up the staircase of Melanie's nail parlor, considering someone had died because of it.

Celia took one slow step after the other, keen to get through with it as she headed to the nail parlor office.

"You look busy," Celia said with a smile as she walked through the door.

She found Melanie deeply engrossed as she stared at her computer screen.

"Just reading our business plan a little as I try to stay on track with things," Melanie replied. "Is Fidel down there?"

"I don't think so. I didn't see him when I walked in. What's going on?" she asked.

"I'm wondering the same thing. He hasn't turned up for work today."

Melanie stood up and walked out. From the landing, she could see the expanse of the nail parlor.

"Has he turned up yet?" Melanie asked, calling out to Sarah below.

"He sent me a message some minutes ago. He's not

going to make it today," Sarah replied.

"Why not?"

"He said he's handling a family matter."

"Is it serious?" Melanie asked.

Sarah shrugged and got back to preparing her workstation.

Melanie tried to call him on her cell phone.

"He's unreachable. I guess it's serious," she said.

"Let me know if he tries to get in touch with you again, okay?" she shouted to Sarah.

Sarah nodded.

Melanie walked back to the office, Celia in tow.

"Did you manage to talk to him the way we had agreed?" Melanie asked Celia.

"I actually didn't. He's a tough nut to crack, so I have to figure out another way," Celia replied.

"He hasn't said anything to me either. When he gets back, please talk to him. Like I told you, I think he knows something that could help me."

"Sure."

"I have another favor to ask you. Can you take me downtown?" she asked.

"What do you need to do downtown?"

Melanie sighed, then locked eyes with Celia. She immediately knew what Melanie was referring to.

"Do you think he'll listen to your case?"

"He has to because I need more time. Our projections and our reality are two different things. It'll take some time to pay him back. Besides, I need you to come with me because you're more persuasive than I am."

"You flatter to deceive, you know that?"

"I'm being honest," she replied.

"I have a question for you. What's your honest opinion about Patricia?" Celia asked.
Melanie thought about this for a minute.

"She clearly doesn't like the fact that we're running a business next to hers. She's got this scheming side to her, but I'm not sure she'd take the risk of getting Charlize killed just to get a piece of this business," she remarked.

"Stranger things have happened," Celia said, "Turf wars don't exist in the drug world alone, you know."

Melanie laughed.

"How's it a turf war and we'd only just began operations?"

"The turf war began the minute you decided to set this place up. Being a new place doesn't matter," Celia replied.

"I know what you mean but I just can't see how she would've done it."

"I think you need to keep an open mind about what could have happened," she urged.

"I'll make note of that. Right now, I really need a ride downtown. Are you in?" Melanie asked.

"Tell me something. How much did you know about this loan shark deal?" Celia asked.

"I honestly knew nothing about it. I didn't know the amount, the terms, the timelines. It seems Charlize was paying them off quietly. Until now," she said.

Celia had experienced loan sharks before, and they gave her goosebumps thinking about the experiences she'd had with them. As she was struggling to get her business off the ground, she needed to buy stock. It was brutal when she didn't pay on time, and she regretted every bit of it. She worried for her friend, because things could get complex quite fast.

"Mel, do you know any of these guys?"

"I know none of them. All I know is the name of the man I owe. Benji."

"Have they threatened you yet?" Celia asked.

"It hasn't gotten to that point yet. Why are you asking me all these questions?" she asked.
"I think you should simply not turn up. You didn't make the deal. Charlize did. She's passed on. They should discuss a new timeline for you."

"I don't think that is a safe bet. Remember, they know where the business is."

"This is going to get a little tricky for you, I'm afraid," Celia said.

"So, you're not going to take me downtown?" Melanie asked.

Celia sighed.

"You know me. There's no way I'll let you go into the lion's den without company," Celia replied with a smile.

They left together. Celia was keen to see what awaited them downtown.

11

Downtown wasn't the seediest part of the town, but it was one of the dangerous ones.
It wasn't a secret that this town had some gangs, and they operated much more freely in the downtown area. Some ran legitimate businesses, but most owned turf where they ran various devious schemes.

As Celia drove through the streets, she could tell her car was being studied by some groups that they drove past.

"Charlize drove down here to meet this guy?" Celia asked.

"I honestly have no idea if she did," Melanie replied.

"Maybe we should've asked to meet him at a restaurant," she said.

"He wanted it this way. So here we are," she clarified.

The address they were told to go to was a brick and mortar high-rise building on a busy street. To Celia's relief, it had a basement parking and she drove down into it. It was well lit, and most of the parked cars were more expensive than hers. This eased her concerns.

They headed to the third floor. The lifts weren't working, so the staircase was the only way up. It was full of human traffic, so it was slow going as they jostled and darted up the steps. The corridor leading to the loan shark's office was full of small offices that ran open door businesses. They had stuck signs and placards advertising all types of services which included mobile phone repairs, a barbershop, electronics, cheap clothing, alcohol among others. It was a testament to the town residents' determined spirit to earn a living. Celia was impressed.

They got to a grilled black metal door. On it was the small piece of wood imprinted, *BCash Investment.*

Inside, a small reception area greeted them. The receptionist, a petite lady, ushered them into the larger office. A muscular man with slicked back hair, the man Celia had seen at the soft launch, was seated on a tall leather seat behind a shiny mahogany desk.

"Welcome, ladies. I've been waiting for this day for quite a while," the man said as he motioned them to take the cushioned visitor seats.

"Hello, Benji," Melanie said. "Thank you for taking the time to meet us."

"I always make time where my money is involved," he said with a wry smile.

"About that. I had a preposition. Can you give us two more months to get this off the ground? My co-founder recently passed on, and I'm trying to get the ship running again," Melanie said.

Benji leaned back in his seat and studied them.

"A deal is only as good as its word," he said.

"I know that, but..."

"There are no buts. You both made a deal."

"What she's trying to say is that she wasn't present at the time, and she might've made a more realistic projection of the timeline," Celia said.

Benji smiled.

"I can see you brought your public relations person to the negotiating table. It doesn't work, most of the time," he said.

"I'm just trying to help," Celia said.

"It doesn't matter. Maybe I wouldn't have listened to your realistic projections, anyway. For me, time is money. More time means I charge you more. Considering what you're saying, you might not be able to pay me more cash for more time," Benji said.

"I'll work really hard to make that possible," Melanie pleaded.

Benji shook his head and leaned forward.

"I don't work alone. I have people who need to eat too. This is how they eat; when clients like you repay on time. Understood?"

"Understood. But I can..."

"I said no buts. The best I can do for you is a twenty-four-hour extension. After that, I come for what's mine."

Melanie and Celia exchanged glances.

"What does coming for what's mine mean?" Celia asked.

"You'll know it when you see it," Benji said ominously.

Celia didn't like the sound of it, but knew the discussion was over.

As they drove back to the nail parlor, Melanie cut a frustrated figure.

"Charlize left me in this mess without telling me. I don't understand it," she said.

"She was ambitious, but this was a little rash on her part. Unless the cash was used for something else."

"It was used in the business. I checked the books just to be sure," Melanie replied.

"So, what are you going to do?"

Melanie sighed as she studied the traffic outside.

"I wish I could rob a bank, frankly."

They drove in silence for a few more minutes.

"What do you need that could boost the parlor's operations right now?"

"I need some product. I don't have the cash flow to get it."

"Listen. How about I supply you with the products you need on credit? Then we can agree on a good repayment plan."

"You would do that?" Melanie beamed.

"Yes, I would. It won't be on Benji's terms though."

"You're a lifesaver, you know that?" she said.

"Don't get too excited. We still need Benji's cash by tomorrow."

The drive became quiet again as they wrestled with the dilemma that was before them. There had to be a way out.

*

"Where do you want me to put these?" Chloe asked as she carried in two small boxes of beauty products.

"Place them at the corner there," Celia replied.

After placing the boxes as instructed, Chloe took a

break.

"I don't know how you managed to convince me to come here, but it's breaking my back now," Chloe said.

"But I know that you have a thing for manicures and pedicures, so why not?" Celia said.

"You know me too well," Chloe replied.

 They both laughed.

"Seriously, thanks for coming through. Melanie's a little stressed right now considering one of her employees has not turned up for the past two days."

"It's all good, I'm all yours. However, from tomorrow I'm only coming in the afternoon. Dad wants some help at the factory. Is that okay?" she asked.

"No problem."

The door opened, and Gloria Langa walked in. She looked graceful as ever, in casual top and khaki pants. She was in sunglasses, which she took off the moment she walked in.

"Hello, ladies," Gloria said.

Celia walked to her.

"Gloria Langa. I can see that you decided to visit us again," Celia said.

"I hear Melanie is back. Can I see her, please?"

"Sure. Let me take you to her office," Celia said.

Celia led her up the stairs to the mezzanine office. They found Melanie on the phone. They sat down and waited.

"Alright I'll get back to you in about half an hour. Thanks," Melanie said as she hung up.

"My name is Gloria Langa and I'm Charlize's half-sister. You're Melanie?" she said.

"Yes, I am. Celia told me about your visit when I was away."

"I was hoping we could talk about my sister, and what plans you have for this place," Gloria said.

"What would you like to know?" Melanie asked.

"There are many things, including how she worked. But the part I'm most interested in is the day she died. What happened?"

Melanie paused briefly.

"I'm also trying to figure out exactly what happened. She had just left my office after a conversation and the next thing I know, she was tumbling down the stairs," Melanie said.

"What kind of conversation did you have?" Gloria asked.

"Just a regular business conversation with a business partner," she replied.

Gloria nodded.

"I see. She didn't show any signs of strange behavior or illness?" she asked.

"No, she didn't. Like I said, I'm trying to wrap my head around what exactly happened that day as well."

"Interesting," she muttered.

"About the business, I believe that her lawyer is now the guardian of her shares. He passed by twice in the last two days to talk about it. I keep him posted about the day-to-day running as we work to get back on our feet," Melanie added.

"Yes, I'm aware. I talk to Michael every day as well. Is there anything you would like to let me know? Something you would like to get off your chest about my sister?" Gloria asked.

Celia was surprised by the question. Melanie frowned in puzzlement.

"I don't exactly get what you mean," Melanie said.

"It's my hypothesis that the conversation you had was a trigger to what happened to my sister."

"Look here, Gloria. I..." Melanie interjected.

"I'm not finished. I believe something happened in this room that day. I'll find the underlying cause of it. I suggest you start putting your affairs in order because you might not be running this business for very long," Gloria said with finality.

"I can assure you I had nothing to do with what happened to your sister," Melanie countered.

Gloria stood up to leave.

"And I can assure you that no one poisons my sister and gets away with it. I would say you can take that to the bank, but I know your financial situation doesn't allow you to do that. So, let's just say I will see you very soon," she said.

Gloria marched out of the office. Celia turned to Melanie, who was looking shell-shocked.

12

"I told you they are hunting for me," Melanie said.

Celia walked up to Melanie and hugged her.

"This is going to blow over. Trust me," she said.

"I did nothing wrong, Cece. Why can't anyone see that?"

Pulling out of the embrace, Celia and Melanie locked eyes.

"You have to believe something will come through. We just need to find the evidence to clear you," Celia said.

"What more evidence do people need? Isn't my word and my background enough?" she lamented.

"It sounds crazy, but your answers tend to add more doubt than clarity."

"What answers?" Melanie asked.

"Why didn't you tell me about the argument?"

"It wasn't important at the time."

"It wasn't important? Your co-founder died, and you didn't care to tell me you had an argument before the cops walked in?"

"I didn't think it had any bearing on the incident, that's what I meant," Melanie said.

"But as you can now tell, it did. I also know that she was giving you a hard time. Thankfully, your staff have not talked about that much."

"It was nothing I couldn't handle," she replied.

"And then there's the possible disappearance of Fidel, which only the two of us know about," Celia said.

"He's sorting out a family situation," Melanie said.

"You really believe that, or that's just a cover story," she posed.

Melanie took a step back, shaking her head. "Are you suggesting I've something to do with Fidel missing work?"

"I'm not suggesting anything. I'm simply saying a lot of things in your version of events aren't adding up."

Melanie stared at Celia. "You don't believe me, do you?"

"I'm not sure what to believe, Mel."

"You don't believe me. Wow."

"Mel…"

"No, it's fine. I just need some time to myself right now. So kindly leave," Melanie said.

"I'm still here working with you… working on this," Celia said, spreading her arms.
"Just go, Cece."

Celia lingered for a few seconds, then walked out of the office.

Before she left, she asked Sarah for Fidel's home address. She knew he lived across town but didn't know his exact residence.

As she walked out into the busy street, Celia knew she had to find Fidel. He knew something, and his disappearance only made this clearer.

When she got home, her argument with Melanie was

still weighing on her.

"Why do you keep biting your upper lip, Cece? Is something the matter?" Audrey asked.

"It's a long story that I can't share right now," Celia replied.

Her mother wasn't the type of person to tell stories of her friend's ongoing involvement in a murder investigation. She'd end up worrying about Celia's safety.

"I have some news for you," Audrey said, "Christie and I finally agreed on a party theme."

"Oh, really?"

"Yes! And this is the list of things we will need to get to make the party work," Audrey said as she handed Celia a list. It was the longest list she had ever seen for a birthday party. They had gone with a blend of yellow and orange for the theme, and the total was double what she had ever spent.

"Ma, he's still a kid. We don't have to use our cash reserves to pay for a birthday party. This budget is insane."

"Who said you're going to pay for it?" Audrey asked.

"Ma, what are you guys going to do, swindle someone?"

Audrey took back the piece of paper.

"Christie and I will cover the costs. As far as we are concerned, you're just a guest," Audrey said as she walked away.

"But they are my kids."

"You're just a guest, Cece. Just a guest."

*

The next day, Celia struggled with her morning deliveries. Her clients noticed she was not upbeat as usual and wondered why. Celia knew the only way to ward off the cloud that was hanging around her was to talk to Melanie. She drove to the nail parlor after her schedule cleared, but it was closed.

She drove to the library and found Melanie at the

reception desk, reading a book.

"Hey, Mel. Can we talk?"

"I don't think we need to do that right now," Melanie replied.

"I'm here to apologize about what I said earlier."

Melanie didn't respond.

"I was wrong. I know there are gaps in your account of what happened, but I had no right to accuse you. I'm sorry," she said.

Melanie closed the book and stood up.

"Come with me," she said as they walked outside.

They stood to one side of the entrance, where Melanie could at least see if anyone walked in or left.

"Don't you value our friendship?" Melanie asked. "Do you think that after all we've done together, including solving a case, that I'd do this? Don't you realize I have too much to lose? I've basically no one to turn to. You're the only person that I could talk to about anything in my life. To hear you say those words hurt me deeply."

"You're right. You have every reason to be

disappointed with me. I'm here to apologize and say that I'm still in your corner. I'm still here to help you find out what happened to Charlize," Celia assured her.

"Are you sure being close to me won't cloud your judgment?" she asked.

"I'm here to find out the truth. It won't break this friendship," Celia said.

Suddenly Melanie's phone rang. It was Sarah.

"You need to come to the parlor right now."

 "It's closed. What's happening?"

"I'm there right now and the door is open. They've come to take your stuff," Sarah said.

"Who are you talking about?"

"Some guys who look like bad news," Sarah replied.

Melanie lowered her phone slowly.

"It's Benji."

When Celia's car skidded to a stop outside the nail parlor, they found a bakkie, a light pickup truck, parked outside the door. Sarah was standing outside with a friend.

"They're inside. I don't know if they are auctioneers or..." Sarah said.

"I know who they are," Melanie said as she and Celia rushed in.

Inside, three men worked to disconnect beauty equipment. One was standing near the door.

"What the hell do you think you're doing? Put that stuff down!" Melanie shouted.

"We're here to collect what you owe," the man said.

"I said stop it!" Melanie shouted again as she tried to grab his arms. He pushed her off easily with his muscular strength.

"You can't do this, please. Please don't do this," Melanie said.

Celia was not going to stand back either. As one of the men tried to carry out a tray full of nail products, Celia stood in front of him. When he tried to move to the side, she moved with him.

"I don't want to hurt you. Please get out of my way," the man said.

"You heard her. You don't have to do this," Celia said firmly.

"If you don't pay, they don't stay," the man said.

"She's going to pay," Celia replied.

"That deadline lapsed. Today's collection day."

Celia braced herself, and then spoke, "I'll give you a choice: you either take those things or you give me twelve more hours to get your money. One of them is going to take weeks for you to make your money back and the other will take just twelve hours. What's it going to be?"

The man glared at her, wondering if she was pulling his leg.

"You realize you're making a deal with people you shouldn't cross, right?"

"I realize that," Celia said, pushing back the fear that was threatening to choke her.

The men exchanged glances.

"Twelve hours is twelve hours. Nothing more. If you dare cross that deadline, we have ways of finding you too, Celia," the man said.

Celia swallowed hard.

"See you tomorrow," the man said. He put down the tray and walked out.

The other men also sauntered out to their pickup truck, jumped in the back, before it sped away.

As Melanie and Celia watched the car drive off, they spotted Patricia watching things from across the street. She had a wry smile on her face.

"She seems to like a scene," Celia said.

"I'm telling you, Cece. Someone on the outside is playing games with us and I wouldn't be surprised if it has something to do with that woman who was staring at us right now," she said.

For once, Celia agreed with Melanie. It was time to find out what Patricia was really up to.

13

When Celia met Melanie at the café, she was a nervous wreck.

"I didn't sleep last night. I think for the first time in my life I got a panic attack," Melanie said.

"You should take some time out to forget about all that's happening around you. Maybe you should focus more time at the library," Celia suggested.

"The issue isn't where I spend time. It's the thoughts in my head. With each passing day I see new enemies and people I care about being sucked into this mess," Melanie lamented.
"You need to keep it together, Mel. For me and for other people who care about you," Celia encouraged her.

Melanie nodded.

"Drink your latte before it gets cold," Celia said.

Melanie sipped on her drink. "Do you think we can find Fidel?" she asked.

"We'll find him, don't worry about it. I'm tracking down where he lives. He seems to be quite a secretive guy, no one seems to know."

"Maybe I should report him missing. I have a photo of him in my staff files."

"No, we can't do that. Let's give it till the end of the day. If I can't trace him and he doesn't show up somewhere, we can consider making a report."

"Why not now? Every minute counts, doesn't it?" Melanie said.

"I know you're worried. He might be the only witness who holds the key to your freedom. But remember you're still a suspect to the police. They might think you've got a hand in his disappearance," she said.

"You see what I mean? It just keeps getting worse and worse," she wailed.

Celia reached out to hold her friend's hand and squeezed it gently.

"It will get better. One day, weeks from now, we'll look back and laugh about this. Trust me," Celia said.

Melanie nodded. "One step at a time."

"Exactly," Celia replied. "For now, we have a meeting with Benji to go to."

Melanie leaned forward. "Cece, you've already done so much for me. You don't have to do this," she said.

"I want to do this. That's what friends are for," she replied.

"Thank you. I hope it's not a meeting downtown, like last time," Melanie said.

"No, thankfully. I asked him to meet us at the park."

"And he agreed to that?"

"He wasn't lying when he said he'll make time for his money," Celia replied.

*

The Bay Gardens Park was the town's best kept secret with a rich wealth of greenery and trees. It was perfect for those who wanted a quick relaxing stroll or for a romantic picnic.

Celia would have loved a picnic, as she watched a squirrel run up a tree. They were seated some meters from the entrance on a bench under the shade of a tree. It was cool and peaceful and even the sound of the highway traffic was filtered away by the lush surroundings.

"This was a good choice," Melanie said. Her eyes were closed as she breathed in the cool park air.

"I sometimes come here in between client meetings. It helps me clear my head and forget the madness of the world."

"It looks like I'll be borrowing that habit and making it my own," Melanie said.

Celia smiled.

Moments later, Benji walked up to them, accompanied by one of his men. The man hung back, scanning the area for any threats.

"Am I early?" Benji asked, smiling like an old friend.

"Not at all. Perfect timing," Celia replied. Melanie had bolted up and they all shook hands.

"I have lived here all my life and have never been to this place," Benji said.

"It does exist. Good for meetings and leisure," Celia said.

"I can see that. It's beautiful, but not my kind of thing. I'm more used to concrete and cash," he replied.

Celia was secretly happy that he wasn't in love with it. She would've never come back to the park if it meant bumping into the loan shark.

"Here's the cash as agreed," Celia said, handing him two thick stuffed envelopes. "All cash as requested."

Benji took the envelopes. He looked around, running his fingers across the edges of the envelopes as he toyed with the idea of counting the cash in the park.

"I trust it's all there. I wouldn't want to feel shortchanged," he whispered.

"I wouldn't do that to you. I'm a woman of my word," Celia reassured him.

Benji smiled. "Great. It was a pleasure doing business with you. All the best with your parlor. And my deepest condolences on the loss of Charlize. She was quite something," he said.

Melanie took a step forward.

"Tell me something, Benji. How did the two of you meet?" she asked.

"I don't remember. I'm not good with that bit of things. She had my number; I had the money she needed."

"Anything else that stood out to you about her?" Benji smiled.

"You're fishing for something. You won't find it with me. Have a great day, ladies," Benji replied. He walked away quickly, his henchman following closely behind.

Melanie turned to Celia with a tear in her eye and said, "Thank you."

When Celia got home, her mother met her in the driveway. She was holding some balloons in her hand.

"This is your ticket into the house. We've just started," Audrey said.

"What's this?" Celia asked.

"It's a balloon halo," Audrey replied.

Celia was confused. "Who came up with this?" she asked.

"Just wear it and enjoy the party," Audrey said.

Celia obliged, squeezing the chicken wire halo that held the two balloons onto her head. It fit just right. She walked into the house. The living room was yellow nearly everywhere and packed with kids in all manner of joyful states. There was chatter, laughter, shrieking, arguments and other displays of innocent child energy. It was infectious.

Celia felt more alive than she had felt for most of that day.

Mrs. Owens and Audrey had put together a very lively birthday party full of all kinds of food and snacks. Instead of Dinosaur Man, they had brought in an actor with a full Minion mascot outfit in yellow and blue. The kids kept adding the mascot in most of their activities, and Celia knew the actor would be exhausted at the end of it all.

On top of all the usual cakes and tasty bites, Mrs. Owens had made low sugar snacks and juices to keep things healthy. Her other highlight was seeing Mrs. Owens and her mother sipping juice while seated together as they enjoyed the kids having fun.

Celia spent a lot of that time serving the children and ensuring her sons were as happy as could be. She was enjoying the distraction. It was a nice break from all the tension. She got her son, the birthday boy, his favorite football team's kit from head to toe. He had recently become very passionate about playing it at school and she wanted him to know he had her full support.

Early the next day, Celia went to see Melanie with a slice of cake from the party. She wanted to check on her before heading for her client delivery trips. Melanie was starting her day at the library, so Celia drove there. She had called in advance and found the front door open. Melanie was performing her early morning duties.

Celia held up the cake jar and waved it at Melanie as she approached. "I've brought the sugar rush you need for today," she said.

Melanie smiled. "I hope you have more because that jar might not be enough for me," she replied.

"My Mum makes heavenly cake. You only need this one because it packs a punch," Celia said.

As Melanie ate the piece of cake, Celia told her how the birthday party went. Then, Melanie's phone rang. It was Patricia.

"I don't need her to ruin my appetite so early in the day," Melanie said.

"We need to know what she's up to. Talk to her. Only

this time, string her along," Celia said.

"String her along?"

"Yes. Make her believe you want the deal."

Melanie nodded. She took the call, putting it on speakerphone.

"Hello, Melanie. How's it going this morning?" Patricia asked.

"I'm fine, thanks. What's on your mind?" Melanie asked, trying her best to be civil.

"You know I'm still thinking about the offer I made you. I want to sweeten the deal a little more. How about I add two thousand dollars. Would that make you reconsider?"

Melanie paused, as if doing a mental calculation of exactly how much investment she had put in. "You know what? If you double that I might be open for conversation," Melanie replied.

Celia gave her the thumbs up sign.

"Let me get back to you on that but I'm happy that you're coming around to the idea. I'm confident that we can come to an agreement. I'll be in touch," Patricia said.

When Melanie hang up, Celia was excited.

"Nicely done. Very believable," Celia said.

"You think she'll buy the place?"

"I think she'll have the money. Once we start talks with her, we can dig into her a little more," she replied.

"What if I actually want to sell the place?" Melanie asked.

Celia frowned. "Are you serious about that?"

Melanie sighed.

"Maybe it's too much trouble to keep the business," Melanie said gravely, "I wouldn't want to end up like Charlize."

"Why are you saying that? Did someone threaten you?"

"Because it might be time to let it go," she said.

"What happened, Mel?" Celia prodded.

"I can't talk about it right now. Thanks for the cake."

With that, Melanie walked off, the echo of her

footsteps sounding hauntingly in the large space.

14

Celia didn't see Melanie for the next two days. They had brief chats on the phone, checking in on each other. Melanie never mentioned if she was in fear for her life, or whether Patricia had called back. Celia judged that her friend needed some time to think. For those two days, the nail parlor was closed. This worried Celia slightly, but she understood. However, if it went on for longer than necessary, she would have to do something to get Melanie back to herself again.

That particular morning, Celia slept in. She had been doing more client visits than normal to make up for the days she had spent attending to the nail parlor and Melanie.

She was woken up by her alarm clock. When she grabbed it to stop its incessant ringing, she was surprised to discover that it was midday. For some reason the clock had rung later than it usually did. She made a note to have it checked in case it was faulty. Checking her phone, she saw a missed call from Detective Bill Koloane.

She hoped it wasn't something to do with the case. She called back.

"Good morning Celia, did I call at a bad time earlier?" he asked.

"Not really. I was asleep, though. Not intentional," she replied.

"Then it was a bad time. I was wondering if you were open for coffee later today," he said.

Celia almost choked. He was finally asking her out. She did a quick calculation of her day. She had already lost a couple of hours. It would be a tricky fit.

"I would've loved to, but I need to catch up with the day. Let me take a rain check on that one," she replied.

"At least I tried. Have a great day and hope to see you around sometime," he replied.
"But not at the station," Celia added.

"Of course. No stations involved," he said with a chuckle.

As she got ready for the rest of the day's activities,

she realized she loved the fact that he had called. It had made her day more exciting.

"Get a grip on yourself, Cece," she said to herself.

A few hours later, she was glad to see the transformation in the face of a satisfied customer.

"You always bring me the best these days. Thank you!" Flavia said as she took her delivery.

"These days? I've always brought you the best, Flavia," Celia protested.

"I know that. But if I tell you that every day, it will go to your head," Flavia countered.
Celia laughed. She probably had a point.

"You're always welcome. Next time, let me know what you need a week early," Celia said.

"You can count on that," Flavia replied.

Celia drove out into the light afternoon traffic. She decided to head to the Pier for a quick lunch before planning her afternoon.

She had just taken a seat when she received a text.

'Are you free?'

It was Melanie.

'For about an hour. Why?' Celia texted back.

'I need a ride. Can you come over?'

'Where are you?'

'At Charlize's funeral. Westmore Cemetery.'

Celia wasn't aware that the funeral was happening that day. She was more surprised that Melanie attended, considering she was one of the suspects in Charlize's death. She hoped that her friend was okay.

'Heading there now. Stay safe.'

*

Westmore Cemetery was the only prestigious burial ground in the area. Usually, the well-to-do were laid to rest there. It had well-manicured lawns, elaborate graves with fancy tombstones, and was well spaced out.

When Celia got there, Charlize's burial seemed to be the only one taking place that day. It had already ended. Mourners had gathered in small groups, talking, while others got into their cars and were driving off. There was a long procession of cars parked close to the burial site.

Celia found Melanie standing near the large oak tree at the corner leading to the burial site. She was dressed in black from head-to-toe, including a pair of dark sunglasses.

 "Thanks so much for coming. You're a lifesaver," Melanie said as she got into the car.

"You have to stop saying that," Celia said.

"Alright, I'll remember next time," Melanie replied as she took off her sunglasses.

"I'm surprised that you're here, considering Gloria is not exactly a big fan of yours."

"I know. I'm still innocent till proven guilty, though. I kept my distance from the immediate family.

Charlize was my friend, despite all her flaws and the tragic way she died," she said.

"Where to now?" Celia asked.

"You can drop me at the library. I'm still not ready to go to the nail parlor right now."

As Celia drove off, she had to pass by the mourners lined up on either side. It was slow going as they snaked their way through.

As they were just about to go past the last group of mourners, a woman in black wearing a wide-brimmed hat, sunglasses and a dark veil over her face walked onto the road and stood in front of Celia's car. It was Gloria.

Celia and Melanie exchanged glances, wondering what was going on.

Gloria walked to the passenger side of the car. Melanie rolled down her window.

"I just wanted to say thank you for coming," Gloria said.

"You saw me?" Melanie asked.

"Of course. It's a very open space here," she replied.

"I just came to pay my last respects," Melanie declared.

"I would like us to have a chat sometime, Melanie. How about tomorrow?" Gloria asked.

"Ummm, sure. Would you like us to meet at a restaurant or something?" she asked.

"We'll meet at the nail parlor. I think that works best for both of us. Say one o'clock?" Gloria said.

Melanie nodded.

"Great, see you then," Gloria said, stepping back.

Celia saw her watching them drive off from her rear-view mirror.

"That was interesting," Melanie said, "Good to see that she didn't take it to heart that I was at the funeral."

"Again, I'm surprised that..." Celia didn't finish her statement.

"Wait, wait! Stop the car," Melanie exclaimed.

"What's going on?"

"Just stop the car, Cece!"

Celia braked hard, relieved that no one was behind her.

"Behind the trees there. Do you see what I see?" Melanie asked.

Celia squinted her eyes.

"It's a guy walking. Wait, is that…"

"It's Fidel. It's him! Come on, let's catch up with him," Melanie said.

Celia quickly turned to the left, away from their driving path out of the cemetery. She joined a narrow lane. As she got closer, Fidel heard their car approach. He started running.

Melanie got her head out of the passenger side window.

"Fidel, please don't run. Don't run!" Melanie shouted.

Just as they lined up with him, he ducked behind a line of trees and disappeared from view.
"Stop the car!" Melanie screeched.

The car had barely stopped when Melanie jumped out and ran towards the crop of trees where he had disappeared. Celia followed closely behind.

When they got to the line of trees near the ridge, Fidel was nowhere to be seen.

Like a ghost, he was gone.

15

"Where did he go?" Melanie asked.

"He must know his way around this place," Celia mused.

They had just spent another fifteen minutes looking around the area to see if they could spot him. His footprints disappeared after the line of trees, masked by the dead leaves spread all over the ground. It would have been easier to track him with a search dog, Celia thought. He was not up in the trees either.

"Let's go. We won't' find him here," Celia said.

They walked back to the car and settled into their seats.

"Let's assess this for a minute. Fidel goes missing. He can't be found. No one knows where he lives. Even on the records you have, right?"

"Right," Melanie replied.

"Okay. So the question is: why did he attend the burial?" Celia asked.

"He was doing what I was doing. Paying his last respects."

"But why was he hiding from the crowd? Just like you?"

"I can't tell," Melanie said.

"Just like you, he's taking precaution. I don't think he was hiding from you. Just like me, he'd be surprised to see you here. There's someone he fears in that group of mourners. Someone close to Charlize. The question is who," Celia said.

"It could be Gloria, other business associates..."

"Or Patricia," Celia said.

"Of course. Patricia," Melanie said.

"Something doesn't add up here," Celia said.

"I got a note the other day."

Celia turned to her.

"What note?"

"It was more of a threat. Or a warning," Melanie said.

"Where is it?"

"I tore it up. I found it at the parlor. Just before I opened the place. Whoever put it there knew what time I opened the place. It simply said that I should stay away from Patricia."

"What does stay away mean? It could be anything."

"Yeah, but I can't take risks to find out what anything means," Melanie replied.

"Is that why you've kept the place closed for the last few days?"

"It's one of the reasons," Melanie replied.

Celia pondered this revelation.

"You told me that you had a photo of Fidel in your staff records, right?" Celia asked.

"Yes. Why? We don't need to report him missing, at least we know he wants to hide," Melanie replied.

"We don't need to do the reporting," Celia said, "I

have a better idea."

*

Melanie was apprehensive, Celia could easily tell.

Whenever Melanie got nervous, she rubbed her wrists. If it was mild, she'd rub her wrists gently and slowly. When it was high level, she'd vigorously squeeze or massage her wrists as if she was trying to wipe off a stain.

They were seated in the nail parlor's mezzanine office. Gloria was sipping on a mug of takeaway coffee that she had come with. Celia was standing next to the windows listening to the conversation.

Celia could also tell that Gloria didn't want her in the room as she talked to Melanie, but Melanie had insisted. She wanted to study her body language and step in if Melanie got overwhelmed. Gloria had obliged.

"I know I came off pretty strong the first time I was here. I hope you can forgive me. I was quite emotional after losing Charlize, so I hope you understand where I was coming from," Gloria said.

"I understand. Grief is a difficult thing to navigate," Melanie replied.

"I'm hoping that we can all recover from this loss," Gloria said, "I know that she played a big role in setting up this business. The two of you working together was going to be very successful."

"Thank you for the kind words," Melanie replied.

"How are you planning to continue the business?" Gloria asked.

"Well, I've got a plan and so far, it's working. Of course, the pace has been slow as we readjust. When I get another partner, it will be a great thing," Melanie replied.

 "So, you're looking for another partner, right?" Gloria asked.

"Yes, but I'm not in a hurry at the moment. I want to pick the right one. We'll make do with what we have in the short term," Melanie said, briefly nodding at Celia.

"That's good to hear. I was going to say that instead of getting a partner, you could actually consider selling off the business perhaps?" Gloria casually said.

Melanie clasped her hands together tightly.

"I don't intend to sell the business," she said firmly.

"I hear you. I just thought that it'd be a great way to honor my sister's memory."

"Why would it be so important to sell it in her memory? I mean, if the wrong person buys it, they'd kill the business," Celia chimed in.

"It was just a suggestion," Gloria said, smiling, "You can actually ignore it. Let's talk about something else."

Melanie smiled back, but it was one borne out of suppressed anger.

"I believe in the business," Melanie said, "It's very important to me, the same way it was important to Charlize when she was alive."

"I don't doubt that. My only concern is you are a library person. This beauty industry business isn't a walk in the park."

"What are you trying to say, Gloria?" Melanie asked.

"Focusing on what you're good at is usually a great way to attain success." she said.

Melanie laughed aloud this time. Again, Celia could tell it was a way of suppressing her anger.

"I'm not interested in having a conversation with you if all you're going to do is insult me. We're done here," Melanie said.

"At least think about it," Gloria said as she stood up and left.

Melanie banged her hands on the table as soon as Gloria was out of earshot.

"What's wrong with that woman? Can't she just grieve in a normal way?" she raged.

"What she said wasn't driven by grief," Celia said.

"What was it driven by?"

Celia pursed her lips. She had keenly studied Gloria's body language throughout the exchange. She knew the weight of what she was about to say.

"Gloria wasn't here to offer you any advice or to make amends. She's still declaring war. Considering this is the second time she's doing this; you need to watch your back."

16

"There's a saying that goes 'if two elephants fight, it's the grass underneath their feet that suffers.' You now have two big elephants circling around you. They will crush you if you let them," Celia said.

"But they're not fighting each other," Melanie said.

"Not directly. They both want you to sell the place for different reasons. Patricia wants the whole of Main Street to herself. Gloria... Gloria maybe needs the money for some reason."
"She doesn't look like it."

"She doesn't have to. Since the proceeds go to the family, she seems primed to be a beneficiary."

"Good thing Charlize and I did the fifty-fifty split."

"You told me you might consider selling it the other day. Then today I saw a side of you that's passionate about the place and I wondered what changed?"

Celia said.

"I was at a low place then. But I want to put up a fight. I've been warned about Patricia. I don't know why they warned me about her. I'm not comfortable dealing with her. Gloria's motives are unclear. Maybe a different buyer would sway me more," Melanie said.

"So, what are you going to do?" Celia asked.

"Hold out until I can't anymore."

"I expect them to try to force you into a deal."

"They just might."

"Then we'll need to prepare for them. Meanwhile, give me Fidel's file. I need to check it out."

"How long do you need it for?"

"Not long. Why?"

"I'm taking the afternoon off, and so will you. Our date is happening this evening," Melanie said.

"Are you serious? Chloe never sent the invite."

"I'm the invite, because we're going there together."

Celia never expected to be listening to a band on a weekday evening.

Of course, she'd done it before, when Trevor was alive. It was their second wedding anniversary. He'd taken her to their favorite restaurant at the time, the *Grass Whisperer*. The band played so beautifully that if he'd proposed to her a second time, she would've said yes. It was one of her favorite memories.

The band playing this evening mixed instrumental songs with acapella versions seamlessly. It was magical, and instantly ushered in a relaxed, carnival atmosphere.

Celia was feeling nostalgic as she sat next to Chloe and Melanie. They each sipped glasses of fruit wine, compliments of the restaurant as they waited for their three dates to arrive.

"Why are we the first ones to get here? Ideally, the men are supposed to be waiting for us," Melanie asked.

"Well, this was a way of throwing them off. They'd have to bring their A-game now when they know we've been waiting for a while," Chloe replied.

"I'm not sure that's a wise decision, but I guess it's never too late to try out something new,"
Celia remarked.

"That's the spirit," Chloe said with a smile, "Cece is ready to take on the challenge. You should warm up to things, Melanie."

Melanie shrugged.

"One thing that will warm me up right now is some roasted steak and potatoes," Melanie countered.

"Be at ease, the wait is ending now," Chloe whispered.

Sure enough, two men approached their table. One was dressed in a navy merino zip neck jumper and khaki pants while the other wore a black shirt with gray trousers. Both looked well-groomed and smiled as they got closer.

They greeted the women warmly and took their seats opposite to their dates, Melanie and Chloe.

"Ladies, this is my date Casper. He's a programmer," Chloe said as she pointed at the zip neck jumper guy, "This other gentleman is George, he's an interior designer."

"Nice to meet you all," George said as Casper waved.

Celia leaned over to Chloe.

"I can safely say that I'm solo, right?" Celia asked

with a smile.

Chloe giggled. "Your date is five minutes late, but he's on his way," she said.

Celia didn't have to wait long. Emerging from the shadows, a familiar figure walked to the table.

Celia didn't want to believe her eyes, but when he finally stood opposite her, she couldn't help blushing.

"I apologize for being late, but I think I could get a warmer greeting," Detective Bill Koloane said, smiling broadly.

Without answering him, she gave him a warm hug.

"You could've warned me it was you," she whispered into his ear.

"I'm just as surprised as you are," he whispered back.

They settled into their seats. When Chloe tried to make conversation that would involve everyone, Celia and Bill inevitably ended up talking to each other more than they did to the rest of the group. She learned a lot about Bill that night: his love for long drives, going outdoors, cycling, traveling, his love for children, his upbringing in a broken family and his love for pastries. Melanie and Chloe occasionally gave Celia knowing looks and winks as the evening wore on.

During dessert, Celia leaned over to Bill and whispered, "Not to be rude, but I honestly wish that we'd go somewhere else and just talk."

"You read my mind," he replied.

Their inside jokes continued for most of the night. By ten o'clock, they were all full, cheerful and ready to go home. Bill insisted on following Celia's car until she got home. When they got to her house, they stood next to her car watching the stars.

"We finally did this," he said.

"I didn't think that it would take Chloe to convince you to make time," Celia replied teasingly.

"I've learned my lesson and apologize."

"I think a true apology involves changed behavior. Can I expect a different approach?" she asked.

"You'll definitely get a different approach," he replied.

They turned to each other and looked into each other's eyes for what felt like an eternity. She wanted to kiss him, but it felt too soon.

"Have a beautiful night," she said, embracing him.

"Sweet dreams, Cece. I can call you Cece now, right?"

"Yes, you can," she said.

As she walked to her front door, she felt like she was walking on a cloud. She heard him drive away and already missed his presence. It then hit her she was falling for a detective. Was she crazy? Trevor was an army man, a man of danger. Bill was a cop, another man of danger. What did that say about Celia? Was her love for dangerous men a good thing or a flaw? She didn't really want to know, not at that moment. This felt good, and she was enjoying every minute of it.

It was when she inserted the key into the lock that she saw the note. It was taped on top of her door. At first it looked like something the boys would've done. When she took it, she unfolded it to see if there was something written inside.

'Stay away from the Melanie situation. It won't end well for you.'

Cold shivers went up her spine and replaced the warm fuzzy feeling she'd enjoyed all evening.

17

Celia was torn.

Part of her wanted to open the door as quickly as possible and lock herself in the house. The other part wanted to search around the house, because whoever had taped the note might be watching. She went with the latter, scanning the dark shadows around her home. She was hoping for some movement, but she spotted none. All she could hear were crickets, the occasional rustling of leaves and passing traffic.

Who was this? How did they know her house? Who was trying to warn her and Melanie and why?

She had many questions as she got into the house. She fastened all the locks and set the house alarm, just in case. Without switching on the house lights, she went to the window and spent another ten minutes watching the shadows outside. Maybe the intruder would feel safe and make a mistake. Again, she spotted nothing.

When Celia got into her bedroom, she saw the feed from her CCTV camera. She rewound the footage for the evening and studied it.

Her mother drove in.

She played with boys in the driveway.

They got back into the house at seven.

At nine o'clock, a dark figure appeared.

The intruder was wearing a hoodie and a facemask, so she couldn't make out who it was. The figure kept close to the house, so it was hard to know their walking style. With no clear identifiers, she knew it was a lost cause. At least she knew what time they'd made their move.

She went into the kitchen where she could switch on the lights and examine the note a little more. It was written using a biro pen, and the handwriting was easily readable. She couldn't tell if it belonged to a male or female, but it was definitely an adult. Then she realized it was written on a store receipt. The receipt date was for the previous night! It indicated the purchase of Swiss roll and a pack of sausages. This was a clue she could use. Most likely the writer of the note had made the original purchase.

She went to her bedroom and switched on her laptop. She searched for the Dully store on the receipt. She watched the mouse spin. Then a list of locations emerged. However, there was only one she reckoned it could belong to - the Dully Corner store across town.

Early the next morning, after dropping the boys in school, she drove across town. She had never been to the Dully district of the town in a long time, and yet it had hardly changed. There were a few modern buildings, but most of the locals kept their simple homes and compounds in the same style from twenty years ago. It was still very relaxed and far removed from the high-traffic areas.

The Dully corner store itself was one of the more modern buildings. Sitting conveniently at the junction of two streets, it had a sizeable car park on its front, which was where Celia parked her car.

She walked in like a regular shopper, scouting the place in case she saw a familiar face. It was well stocked with all kinds of essential items, the kind of store that had one or two attendants manning it. She was also checking to see if they had CCTV cameras. They did.
Armed with her can of baked beans, she went to the counter. It was not a busy morning, which was a good thing. After the cashier had checked her out, she made her move.

"Sorry to bother you, but I was here last evening and there's a gentleman who pickpocketed my purse. I only realized this later that night. Could you help me find him?" Celia asked.

"I'm sorry, lady, it's against company policy to do so," the cashier replied.

"Please. He took some cash that I needed to pay for my son's treatment. I know the money will never come back, but at least let's get him off the streets,' Celia pleaded.

There was no one else in the store, and after a moment, the cashier caved in.

They went to a desk close by which had a computer monitor showing the various cameras inside the store.

"You were here at what time?" the cashier asked.

"At seven-o-eight in the evening. Check the counter cameras, because I think that's when he took it," Celia replied.

As they skimmed through the footage, she prayed she would see him without a hoodie. It wasn't likely he would have one considering it would be suspicious in a store, but the skeptic in her wouldn't give herself too much hope.

"There you go," The cashier said, "Did you say seven-o-eight?"

"Yes. Is that him?"

"I don't think so. That's just Fidel, he comes here all the time. It can't be him because I know him."

"You say he comes here all the time?" Celia asked.

"Every evening. Pretty cool guy. Are you sure you were pickpocketed at the cashier's? Because I can't see…"

The cashier turned around to see Celia dart out of the door, heading fast to her car. As she got in, she could hear him shout at her. He wouldn't call the police, she figured. There was nothing really to report there. Just a confused woman who distracted him.

But she had gotten what she wanted. She had seen his face. It wasn't covered by a hood.
It was a familiar face.

It was Fidel!

As she drove away, Celia called Melanie.

"I've found him," Celia said, excitement etched in her voice.

"Found who?" Melanie asked.

"Fidel. I've found him!"

"That's great! Where is he? Have you talked to him?"

"He's not here physically but I know how to get him."

Celia was already thinking of how she would confront him. She needed to do it soon.

"Can I tag along?" Melanie asked.

"Not on this ride, but I'll keep you posted," she said.

"Please do. I'm trying to get Patricia off my back. She has the money and wants to close the deal."

"String her along as much as you can," Celia said.

"I've got to. Thanks for the good news."

As she hung up, Celia knew she only had one shot at this. She would have to make her move that very night, lest he disappeared again.

*

"You know this isn't an actual date, right?" Celia said as she grabbed another beef biltong, the dried meat snack of choice in her town.

She was seated in Bill's police car, interrupted by the occasional chatter from the police radio.

"But it's a sign of changed behavior," Bill said with a smile, "There was no time to ask you out considering the nature of what I do. So here I am."

"I appreciate the effort," Celia said, "although it danced on the edge of reason."

"How so?"

"You saw me in traffic and pulled me over," she said.

"I didn't use my siren. I asked you like any regular guy would. By flashing my headlights."

"Regular guys pick up girls using their headlights?" Celia asked.

"You'd be surprised by what happens in the real world."

They both laughed.

"I just never expected to eat a meal in a police car. At least that's a new memory."

"Which other crazy car have you eaten in?"

"An army tank."

"You're kidding, right?" he exclaimed.

"No, I'm not. I was married to an army guy, remember?"

"Of course. You had some good times, I can imagine," he said.

"Yes, we did. This is a good time too," she said.

"I'm here to create more good times. If you'll be open to that possibility," he replied.

Celia smiled. She understood now. She liked the idea of dating someone who looked for answers, just like she did. It wasn't really about them being a detective or army guy. They looked for answers through the lens she did. This was what attracted her to Bill. She had tried dating two years after Trevor's death, but this was the closest she had come to actually liking someone romantically. It felt like she was twenty-one again.

"I think there's some room for exploration," Celia replied.

"That's sounds like music to my ears," Bill said.

They talked for close to an hour. When it was finally time to go their separate ways, neither of them wanted to say goodbye.

It was almost sunset when she completed her last delivery. She would normally head straight home afterwards, but Celia had some unfinished business.

She had parked some distance from the Dully corner store. She was staking out Fidel. She kept looking at her watch as she counted down towards seven o'clock.

It was soon dark, and the streetlights and car park lights illuminated the area around Celia's car. She was glad.

At quarter past seven, she spotted Fidel's dark, familiar form as he walked into the store. He looked calm and relaxed. This was clearly a place he felt safe. He even didn't feel the need to change his regular routine every evening. She felt lucky. She'd played out the scenario in her mind several times during the day and hoped it would work.

Ten minutes later, he got out of the store. He was

biting into a hotdog as he walked.

"Fidel, we need to talk," Celia said as she suddenly appeared in front of him.

He lost grip of his hot dog, almost dropping it before catching it just in time.

"Please don't run this time. I got your warning note on my front door. I need you to tell me what's going on," Celia said.

Fidel composed himself.

"I shouldn't be talking to you and you shouldn't be here," he said.

"I need to know what's going on, Fidel. Please," she persisted.

Fidel sighed as he tried to think of what to say to her.

"We can't talk here," he finally whispered.

"I've got my car with me. We can drive to wherever you need us to go," she offered.

He hesitated, then nodded.

"Okay. But prepare yourself mentally. It's going to

be a long drive."

18

Driving at night was not something Celia enjoyed very much. Especially when she didn't know where she was going or how long the trip would take.

They had driven out of town and were now on the highway parallel to the beachfront. It did offer great views of the city lights in the distance, but this wasn't that kind of drive.
Fidel kept looking over his shoulder to see if they were being tailed. She found it a little over the top, but she didn't know what story he was about to spill. Maybe the precaution was justified.

They drove for half an hour before he instructed her to take a side road. It was a gravel road with a harsh ride due to the potholes, but she kept going. As she drove, her phone started ringing. It was her mother. She had left her in charge of the boys, knowing it might be a late night. She always told her where she was going to be, but tonight she hadn't. She knew her mother was worried.

"Hey, Ma. How are the boys?" Celia asked, speaking through the Bluetooth in the car. It allowed her to focus on the road.

"They're fine. They just had dinner."

"Great. Tell them I'll be coming in later. If they sleep before I get there kiss them goodnight for me."

"Where are you, Cece? It sounds like you are driving in a rally or something."

She hadn't realized the road was making the car shake and rattle so much.

"I'll update you when I get to my destination."

"You promise to let me know?"

"I promise, Ma."

When she hung up, there was a brief silence before Fidel broke it.

"We're here."

They stopped at the edge of a little township. You could see it in the valley below from where they had stopped, with little lights coming through the widows.

"Where are we going?"

"To have dinner," Fidel said.

"Is the car safe here?"

"Once you've come this far, no one can touch you," Fidel replied.

A short walk from her car led them to a little restaurant that served local cuisine. It was made of recycled wooden pallets taken from freight containers. This gave its exterior a distinct style, although she couldn't appreciate it fully since it was nighttime. On the inside, the decor was simple. The pallets were everywhere, from the chairs to the tables, to the wall art.

"What is this place?" Celia asked.

"It's a hotel. Or as you call it in your side of the world, a restaurant," he replied.

"I mean this whole area?"

"It's called Diskerp. Don't look for it on a map, you won't find it. It's what we call off the grid."

"It can't be really off the grid. I could see those little lights in the township valley."

"Solar power. We have our own solar farm some meters from here. It's dark, so you can't see it."

"Are you serious?"

"Very serious. This is home."

"You commute from Main Street all the way here, every day?" Celia asked.

"No, I have a second home closer to the office. But this is where I call home," Fidel replied.

The waiter, a burly middle-aged bearded man, walked up to them.

"I think I'll order a bunny chow for both of us. You must be hungry."

"I sure am, but I wouldn't finish a full one. Besides, you just had a hot dog not too long ago," Celia said.

"Quarter loaf it is. One each. Thanks," Fidel said.

"And some mineral water, please," Celia chimed.

Fidel smiled.

"You can take chicken broth instead? It's a good substitute," he suggested.

Celia hesitated.

"Alright, with some broth," she said. The waiter nodded and left.

"Why do you love this place?" Celia asked.

"Because there are no CCTV cameras around and they have great food," he said with a smile, "Keeping my tracks invisible doesn't mean I can't have some of the best local food in town."

The food didn't take long. The waiter was back with the bunny chow made out of hollowed out bread filled with curry and strips of chicken. The broth came steaming, ideal for the chilly night.

"First we eat, then we talk," Fidel said.

True to his word, the bunny chow was delicious. It was rich with flavors as if made from the love of a mother for her children. By the time she was on her last morsels, she was too full.

"That was quite something," she said.

"It's the ultimate soul food, I believe," Fidel said, smiling with pride.

Celia noted that this was the most open, sincere version of Fidel she had ever met. Still, she knew he possessed some facts that could just be the key to unlock this murder mystery and reveal who Charlize's killer was. She just hoped she had the right skills to elicit this information from him.

"So, tell me, why did you look for my house and put a note on it?" Celia asked.

"I wanted you to be safe from them. I wanted to stay anonymous, too," he said.

"Who are them?" she asked.

He cleared his throat and spoke.

"I used to work for Patricia Nesbitt, the lady who owns the other nail parlor down the street."

Celia almost choked on her broth.

"You what? For how long did you work for her?"

"Two years," he replied.

"Did Charlize and Melanie know about this?"

"Charlize did. She's the one who hired us."

"So why did you send a note warning Melanie about Patricia? How is Patricia connected to what you want to tell me?"

"After I left, I kept in touch with my colleagues who still work there. They tell me Patricia has been saying a few suspicious things about Charlize's passing."

Celia's eyebrows went up.

"What kind of things are you talking about?" she asked.

"She's saying that she knew that Melanie's nail parlor wouldn't last. She wanted to buy it out. That it was only a matter of time before something tragic happened. You know, crazy stuff," he said.

Yet, to Celia, this didn't sound like something sinister.

"Is there anything else that she said?" she asked.

"After the boss fell down the stairs, she kept telling her staff that Charlize was poisoned. They came and told us."

"But this was already after the police came, right?" Celia asked.

"No, this before the cops came to tell you or Melanie. This was the very day she was poisoned," Fidel said.

This revelation lit a bulb in Celia's mind.

"That's definitely suspicious. Sounds like she knows something we don't," she mused.

"That's exactly what I thought," he said

"So why did you go into hiding?" Celia posed.

"I needed to. Something my boss didn't know about me is that I've been locked up before," Fidel said.

"You mean…"

"Yes, I've been to prison before. I did three years for vandalizing someone's property. I was part of a wrong crowd back then, and we did a few things I'm not proud of. But I thought that the moment the police knew that I, an ex-con, was working at the parlor, they might suspect me. I don't need that kind of attention in my life right now," Fidel replied.

Celia took a moment to take in all the things he had said.

"But you're a good man, Fidel. You're clearly looking out for me. You tried to save Charlize. You even warned Melanie about Patricia."

"Maybe she thinks it's a prank or something," he said.

"She didn't. Especially after you sent me a similar

message as well."

"I just did what I had to do. There are some evil people out here. You never know who's aiming for you," Fidel said.

"You believe Patricia knows something about Charlize's death?" Celia asked.

"When Patricia speaks, she's looking to light a fire. She's not speaking from a rumor mill. She knows something because she was already talking about the poison thing even before the police had announced it to anybody. I would have loved to find out more, but I can't put myself in a situation where I'm digging up that information. I may get myself in trouble," he said, looking around to see if anyone was eavesdropping on their conversation.

Celia listened, dumbstruck that all the things he was saying seemed to be legitimate. She needed to crosscheck his records. But so far, he sounded authentic.

"What if I helped you avoid that trouble? Would you help me find out more from Patricia?" she asked.

"How are you going to do that exactly?" he asked.

Celia smiled. "Fidel, I was able to find you from a store receipt. A receipt, of all things. I didn't even use fingerprints or tracking your mobile phone. I know you're taking precautions with avoiding CCTV cameras, but if I could find you from a receipt, then they can find you just as fast. I've got a friend in the police department who can help us. But I need you to take a risk," she said.

Fidel pondered for a moment. "If I do this, then I have a lot more to lose," he said.

"We both have a lot to lose. But we're here in a wooden restaurant talking about doing the right thing. We can't hide in fear, because this isn't going away if you don't do something. We already lost Charlize. We don't have to lose Melanie or anyone else."

Fidel nodded. "Alright. Let's get them," he said.

19

Celia got out of Diskerp with Fidel in the passenger seat and dropped him off when she had reached a safe distance.

"If you weren't with me, I wouldn't be able to guarantee your safety," Fidel said.

They agreed to keep in touch. He gave her a mobile phone number that he'd only switch on at midday every day, if she needed to reach him.

"Let's keep doing this until we've resolved the situation," he said.

Celia drove as fast as she could, heading home. Her mother was still awake, and Celia had let her know that she was safe and on her way. This wasn't enough for Audrey, so she kept calling every ten minutes for an update.

When she finally did get home, some minutes after midnight, her mother was full of gratitude.

"I thought we talked about this. You're not supposed to be sending me to an early grave, Cece," Audrey lamented as Celia settled in, taking off her jacket and scarf.

"We said that I should keep in touch. You know that it's not always possible to send you my exact location," Celia said.

"Why not?"

"Don't worry, Ma. I'll always be here when you need me, okay?" Celia said. She kissed her mother on the forehead.

They soon bid each other goodnight and retired to their beds.

However, Celia couldn't sleep. Her head was buzzing with ideas. The more she replayed what Fidel had told her, the stronger her resolve became. The wheels in her mind began hatching a plan that might just work.

*

Celia scheduled only one delivery of the new nail polish brand the next morning. After it was done, she called Melanie.

"Tell me something happened," Melanie began.

"Something did happen. I met him. We talked about many things. I can tell you this as fact: he gave us the ticket to clearing your name."

"Yes! I knew it. Tell me more. When is he coming over to talk to the police?" Melanie asked.
"That's the tricky part. He's not going to do that."

Melanie went quiet for a brief moment.

"Why not? How is this supposed to help me?" she asked.

"Calm down, Mel. This situation affects other people too, including Fidel. That's why he went underground. He needs us to help him," she said.

"What do we need to do?"

"I want us to go together and have a chat with our suspicious friend, Patricia Nesbitt," Celia said, "Are you free right now?"

"I'm always free where clearing my name is involved," Melanie said.

"Where are you now?"

"At the nail parlor," she replied.

"Wait for me, I'm on my way there," she said.

She hung up and stepped on the accelerator.

When Celia arrived at the nail parlor, she quickly parked her car and ran inside.

She found Sarah alone.

"Where's Melanie?" Celia asked.

"She left ten minutes ago," Sarah replied.

"Where did she go?"

"She didn't say. All I know is she left in a hurry."

Celia took out her phone and tried calling her. The phone rang, but she wouldn't take it.

"Which direction did she go? Was she in a car?"

"She was on foot. She headed to the right, down the street."

Celia immediately knew where Melanie was headed.

"Oh no, Mel. You're not supposed to go there alone," Celia turned on her heel and dashed out.

She walked past her car, walking briskly down the street. Three minutes later, she stood outside Bittos, Patricia Nesbitt's nail parlor. She had never paid attention to it until now. Even as she rushed to get inside, she couldn't help noticing the red facade with the name emblazoned on top of the door. It felt like a nightclub rather than a nail parlor.

When she walked in, it was reasonably busy. Staffers in red branded shirts were attending to clients. It was definitely a busier morning than AfroStar was having.

One of the staffers available approached Celia.

"Hello ma'am. What kind of service would you like?" she asked in a sweet voice.

Sorry, but I'm not here to get your service. I'm here to see Patricia Nesbitt, your boss," Celia said.

"She's in a meeting right now. Can I ask you to wait

or leave a message?"

"I can't wait nor leave a message. I need to see her. Now," she insisted.

"I'm sorry, I can't let you do that."

"Where is her office?" Celia asked as she walked towards the back of the establishment.

"I'm sorry I can't…"

"Tell me, where is her office?" Celia prodded.

The woman pointed towards the left, where there was a brown metal door.

Celia walked to it. As soon as she got to the door, she could hear the sound of shouting coming from inside.

She felt the knob, and it turned. She barged in. She found Melanie and Patricia glaring at each other. It was clear that they were in the middle of an argument.

"I hope you've come for your friend here, because she's trying to get herself in trouble," Patricia said.

"The wicked run even when they're not being pursued. Do you have something to say to me, Patricia?" Melanie raged.

She was spoiling for a fight. Celia knew a buildup of frustration had led to Melanie's rash action, but she had to find a way to use to it to their advantage. Celia shut the door behind her.

"Even if I had something to say, you're the last person I'd tell it to," Patricia said, holding firm.

"That wasn't a problem when you wanted to buy my parlor, was it?"

"Enjoy saying that because things are changing very fast. You won't see what hit you when it comes," Patricia said.

"Ahh. What are you planning next?" Melanie asked as she stepped up to Patricia.

Celia decided to speak.

"The two of you need to ease off each other," she said.

"No easing off here, Cece. She knows more than she's telling us. I'm here to make sure that she talks," Melanie said with conviction.

"I'm not telling you a single word," Patricia countered.

"We could've done this the easy way, but I guess

we'll have to do it the hard way," Melanie hissed.

With that, Melanie grabbed Patricia by the neck and pushed her towards the wall at frightening speed.

20

In a fraction of a second, the story of the cornered cat flashed across Celia's mind.

The cat could be taunted, but it always made an effort to avoid confrontation. However, when it was pushed to the wall, with nowhere to go, it became vicious.

As she watched Melanie drive Patricia towards the wall, she knew that the cat in this case was Melanie, not Patricia. She had watched her life crumble around her for the last couple of weeks, and she was being pushed to a corner. Now that she had no options left, she had become vicious.

With quick reflexes, Celia pulled off Melanie from Patricia, separating the two women. Thankfully, Patricia didn't' move to attack Melanie in retaliation. It would've overwhelmed Celia.

"Calm down or else you'll lose it all," Celia urged Melanie.

"You have no idea what's at stake," Melanie said.

"I know exactly what's at stake. Now you'll either let me help you or go to prison. What's it going to be?" Celia asked.

She could feel the fight leave Melanie's body as her breathing eased.

"Thank you. Now, let me do the talking from here onwards, okay?"

Melanie nodded.

Celia turned to Patricia, who was standing as she massaged her bruised neck.

"Before you get any ideas, we need to talk."

"I said I'm not saying a word," Patricia replied.

"It's not a request," Celia said. She pulled over one of the visitor chairs and pointed at it.

"Sit!" Celia ordered.

Patricia gingerly eased herself into the seat.

"This isn't an interrogation. This is a conversation. We're not interested in violence, despite my friend's passionate reaction. We just want honest answers to simple questions. Fair enough?" she said.

"I'm going to do a lot of listening. I'm not interested in…"

"Why did you tell your staff that Charlize had been poisoned before the police even knew it?" Celia asked.

"What? She knew that?" Melanie asked.

"Be calm, Mel," Celia snapped. Melanie retreated.

"I don't know what you're talking about."

"Are you sure about that? Because as it stands, Charlize died. No one knew it was because of poisoning except you. What do you think the detectives will say?"

"I didn't do it," Patricia protested.

"It doesn't matter, does it? All they need is to connect these bits of information to its source. You."

"You can't make it stick," Patricia said.

"True, that's not my job. My job here is nearly done. All they need to do is arrest you. Guess who you'll see on the witness stand that day? Five of your employees. Some of them are still working here, but they can't stand for an injustice. You still think I can't make it stick?"

Patricia began visibly sweating. Celia had her where she wanted her.

"We're waiting for your decision," Celia said.

"I'm not the one who did it. But I know the person who might know about it."

"Who?"

"Will you protect me?"

"It depends if you're lying or not. Who?"

Patricia was clearly struggling to say the truth. But she also wanted to save her own skin. The ultimate dilemma.

"Gloria knows something about it."

"Her half-sister?" Melanie asked.

"Yes, her half-sister."

"Stop being outrageous," Melanie said.

"Let her speak, Mel. Tell us what you mean," Celia breathed.

"I don't know much. Just that Gloria knew her sister would be poisoned," Patricia said.

"Who did the poisoning? Where and when did it happen?" Celia asked.

"I don't know!"

"This isn't looking good for you," Celia said.

"That's all I've got to give," Patricia replied.

"So, what's the connection between you and Gloria?" Celia asked.

"She's a silent partner."

"Partner in what?" Celia probed.

"In several businesses, including Bittos," Celia chuckled.

"Hold on. So you're telling me you've been trying to buy our nail parlor on behalf of Gloria?"

Patricia hesitated, and then nodded. Celia and Melanie exchanged looks.

"Suddenly a lot of things make sense. Maybe one more thing that could help you is if you take us to the ringmaster," Celia suggested.

"What do you mean?" Patricia asked.

"Take us to Gloria. Let her speak for herself."

"I can't do that. No way."

"Shall we make the case against you or her? Because we'll win either of those cases. Your choice," Celia said.

Patricia rubbed her eyes. Celia wasn't sure if she was wiping off crocodile tears or real tears.

"Alright, I'll do it. On condition that I'm protected."
"On condition that we find the real murderer, the possibilities remain open."

"I'll give you who you want."

Celia's heart skipped a beat. She couldn't wait to see and hear from Gloria Langa.

A few minutes later, Celia was driving with Patricia and Melanie in the backseat.

Celia preferred it that way because Melanie could keep an eye on Patricia, just in case she tried something funny.

Patricia would occasionally give directions as they headed towards Gloria.

According to Patricia's directions, they were heading towards Gloria's house which was in the Neddle suburb. It was quite a wealthy neighborhood with high gates, electric fences and trimmed hedges.

After forty minutes of driving, Patricia said, "We're here."

To the side of the high brass gate was an intercom system to alert the owner of the house that there were guests at the gate. Patricia spoke into the system.

"Hello, Pat! What brings you here?"

"Sorry to bother you, Glo, but I had something really urgent to discuss."

"It's that serious, huh? Okay. But the automatic gate has a problem so my grounds man is coming to let you in," Gloria replied.

"Sounds good," Patricia replied.

Two minutes later a scrawny young man in a straw hat opened the large gates and they drove in. Celia drove down a driveway that wasn't too long as she could see the main house ahead of her. A well-manicured compound flanked it, with tall majestic trees lining the driveway. Gloria clearly lived well.

The main house was equally majestic, with marble walls and wrought iron windows. Gloria herself emerged to welcome them. She initially looked surprised, but quickly composed herself.

"It's lovely to have you," she said as she led them in.

A tall hallway with art pieces along the walls welcomed them at the door. Her living room had a modernist take to the furnishing. It had modern Scandinavian style seats with trim finishes that gave the room a simple yet sophisticated feel.

Celia loved it.

Once they were all seated and served with fresh orange juice, Celia remembered to discreetly turn on her phone audio recorder.

"So, what brings you here?" Gloria asked.

"I think you're aware I've been pursuing a business deal with…," Patricia began.

"We've come to talk business," Melanie interjected.

"Are you talking about the nail parlor?" Gloria asked.

"Both nail parlors," Melanie replied.

Gloria looked at Patricia quizzically.

"They know, Gloria," Patricia said.

"What do you mean they know?" Gloria asked.

"They know that you're my silent partner."

Gloria let out cheeky laugh, as if Patricia had said a stale joke.

"So what does that have to do with your visit?

Because I don't see how that's anyone's concern. Why have you brought them here?"

"Because she had to," Melanie said.

"Last time I checked, Patricia was a free-thinking person. Why is Melanie replying on your behalf Patricia?"

"This is bigger than her. This is about your half-sister, the dear friend that I lost," Melanie said.

"She was my sister, so I lost someone who might matter more to me than to you," Gloria countered.

"Did she really matter to you Gloria?" Celia asked.

"I beg your pardon?"

"Charlize. Did she really matter to you?" Celia asked

again.

"She was my half-sister, why wouldn't she matter to me?"

"Because I'm sitting here wondering why you would poison your half-sister," Melanie replied.

Gloria's demeanor changed to a more serious and grave expression.

"Are you listening to yourself? Have you come here to insult me in my own home while drinking my own juice?" Gloria fumed.

"She simply asked a very straight forward question which all of us would like an answer to. Did you poison your sister?" Celia asked.

"I did no such thing. I don't know who'd do such a thing," Gloria replied.

"Then why is it that the day after you had an argument at a family meeting about how well she was doing with the nail parlor, she suddenly turns up dead two days later?" Celia posed.

"What happens in my family is none of your business. I'm actually about to have all of you thrown out of my home," she said.

"Patricia told us that Gloria didn't like the fact that Charlize opened the nail parlor on Main Street."

"It was my street. The street with sufficient traffic to cater to one nail parlor. Not two. It didn't make business sense for her to open a competing parlor so close to the one we had started," Gloria explained.

"And that's why you're angry," Celia said.

"Of course, I was angry! It was a silly business decision."

"Where were you the morning Charlize died?" Celia asked.

"I was horse riding at a nearby ranch," Gloria replied.

"Do you have evidence of this?"

 At this point Gloria went quiet as she glared at the three women.

"You're really asking me for evidence?" Gloria asked.

"Yes! If it's not too much to ask," Celia replied.

Gloria stood up. "I'll get you the receipt that I was given that day."

She marched towards the corridor, her footsteps

disappearing into the expanse of the house. It was after two minutes that Celia got the gut feeling that Gloria wasn't coming back.

Celia got up and followed the route Gloria had taken down the hallway. She was passing one of the big windows when she spotted Gloria's form running towards the garage.

"She's getting away," Celia said as she dashed to the front door.

She eventually caught up with Gloria, who had just opened the garage door to reveal three luxurious cars.

"I didn't do anything!"

"Then why are you running? Celia asked.

"You can't arrest me, so leave me alone!"

"She can't arrest you, but I can," Detective Bill Koloane emerged from one end of the garage with two other officers.

"Who are you?" Gloria asked.

"Your ticket to justice," the detective replied firmly as he took out his handcuffs.

21

The Pier was buzzing that afternoon.

It was packed with clients looking for good food and an easy time with their company. Celia, Chloe and Melanie were part of the crowd, talking through how events unfolded.

"She might get bail, but she'll have to put up a strong case for it to be approved. She tried to run," Celia said.

"But she didn't escape," Chloe said.

"It's the intent sometimes," Celia replied.

"But why did she do it?" Chloe asked.

"I think it's easier to ask how she did it."

"Alright, let's go with that," Chloe said.

"Gloria found out that Charlize was opening a nail parlor on the same street. These two sisters never got along since childhood, and that has spilled over into their adult lives. Gloria hated this. She bought some poison, put aside a lethal dose. She then went ahead to ask for a coffee date with Charlize."

"So, she started this plan some weeks before the nail parlor was launched?"

"Yes. She wanted to apologize for the painful memories they shared and the pain they caused each other. Charlize thought it was worth a shot to repair their relationship. But when she went to the washrooms, Gloria placed the poison into her drink. After sipping the drink, she only had two hours to get the antidote."

"Two hours she didn't have," Melanie said.

"Is all this based on what she said?"

"Not entirely," Celia said, "They found CCTV footage from the restaurant where they met. You can see Gloria putting the powder into Charlize's drink."

"So, it caused a heart attack after I stressed her with an argument," Melanie said.

"She was going to have one, anyway. The truth is that by the time she fell down the stairs, she was already dead," Celia replied.

"She's going away for a long time," Chloe said.

"Cece, I wanted to ask you something," Melanie said.

"Sure. What's on your mind?" Celia asked.

"I'm really grateful for all the times you came through for me during this crazy ordeal. You're the true friend that I never thought I needed. Thank you for standing with me," Melanie said.

"Like I said last time, that's what true friendship is all about. Standing in the gap, right?" Celia replied.

"Exactly," Melanie replied. "So, when I say this, I'm not trying to burden you with more responsibility or trying to get off mine. Would you like to be my partner in this business?"

"You're talking about the nail parlor?"

"What other business do I have? The money you gave to pay the loan shark can be considered equity invested. Unless you have misgivings about that."

Celia thought for a moment.

"It was part of my family savings," she said.

"I can understand if you still want it back, but of course we'd have to discuss a payment plan across the next couple of months and…"

"Wait, I wasn't finished. Despite that, I still have an interest in investing part of that money and this could be a good start."

"Is that a yes?" Melanie asked.

"Yes Melanie Dawes, I'll be your business partner. You need to talk to that lawyer though."

"Don't worry. All that has been arranged."

"Fantastic!"

"Why are you using my words?" A voice said.

Celia turned to see Detective Bill. He was holding a bouquet in his hand.

"Hello, detective," Melanie said with a smile.

"Hello, Melanie. Sorry to interrupt you, but I have a package for someone."

Bill handed the flowers to Celia. It was a healthy bunch of red Barberton daisies. Celia was simply astounded.

"I hope you're not allergic to these," he said.

"Not at all. I love flowers," she replied.

"Great. Then you'll like the second gift too."

Celia's eyes widened.

"What second gift?" Celia asked curiously.

"The gift of me. Will you go on a date with me?" he asked.

Celia heard the hushes and giggles around her as her friends watched.

"Yes, I'll go on a date with you, Detective," Celia replied, smiling.

"Drop the name 'detective' as a change in behavior. Deal?" he said with a grin.

Celia chuckled. She liked where this was going.

The End

New Nails and a Nasty Nightmare

Afterword

Thank you for reading Eyebrows and Evil Looks! I really hope you enjoyed reading it as much as I had writing it!

If you have a minute, please consider leaving a review on Amazon or the retailer where you got it.

Many thanks in advance for your support!

MAKEUP AND MAYHEM
CHAPTER 1 SNEAK PEEK

Selling makeup is easy when your client is desperate. This desperation might be due to an impending landmark event, a desire to impress or simply the need to replenish an exhausted supply. Either way, the exchange of cash for goods is much quicker when the common denominator of desperation is in play. Celia Dube was a master at discerning the varied manifestations of this desperation and was equally adept at offering the solution. She had been a beauty consultant and makeup distributor in the Cape Town suburb of Oasis Bay for the last twelve years.

As Celia watched her older son running around the kitchen that morning, she was glad she didn't have the pressure that a nine-to-five job brought to a large percentage of the working population.

"You can't wear the Superman cape to school today!" Celia said to her nine-year-old son James, who was giggling as he ran rings around the kitchen island, his arms stretched in front of him like a superhero cutting through the air at thirty-five thousand feet. She timed his run and swooped him up into her arms. As James wriggled playfully, Celia undid the cape strap around his neck and took it off.

She placed him back on the floor and straightened his slightly ruffled school shirt.

"So when will I wear it?" James asked. He was a charmer, with tiny beady eyes and dimples when he smiled that she often found disarming.

"We'll do that over the weekend at the beach, okay, sweetie?" Celia replied. "Go get your brother away from the TV so we can leave," she added, satisfied that he was fully dressed up.

Celia watched James run into the living room that was painted with the orange rays of morning sunlight. His younger brother John was engrossed with his favorite cartoon, all smiles and focus. So caught up was he that when James called out his name, John didn't even flinch.

Celia reached for the remote control atop the kitchen island, which she kept close for moments like these, and switched the television off.

"Oh, Mom! It was almost finished!" John spun around to look at his mother, wearing his best version of a frown. The boys were pretty good actors, Celia always observed.

"No, it wasn't baby. Come on, we're running late for school. You will catch up in the evening, okay?"

"Promise?" John asked with puppy eyes.

"I promise," Celia replied, with one hand over her heart. John's wide smile returned. Now bounding with energy, John ran towards the front door.

"Come get your backpacks first!" Celia said as she reached for two little backpacks placed on the kitchen stools: a rugged, small khaki one for James and a new blue one for John. Her husband Trevor, a hulk of a man who served in the military, had used the khaki bag to carry daily essentials during one of his military missions in East Africa. When Trevor left it behind as he went on his last tour of duty, James had claimed it and made it his school bag, discarding the new bag she had bought him.

It had been five years, and the khaki bag had seen better days, but James would never think of getting another one. Celia didn't even want James to change it because she loved the memories of Trevor that it brought back.

John got to his backpack first, grabbing it just as James arrived. It had become a competition, as it always was with boys.

"Be careful!" she said for the umpteenth time that

morning.

James slung his backpack faster than his younger brother and pretended it was now a jetpack, resuming his 'fly-through-the-air' antics to get to the door first. He opened the door, and John walked through it before James could squeeze past. Amused, Celia quickly grabbed an apple from the fruit bowl, as well as her car keys, and followed them out.

They emerged into a sunny Cape Town morning as the sun peered out through the tall trees surrounding their home. She loved the fact that they were in the suburbs, away from the skyscrapers and the concrete of the city center. When Trevor had suggested making their family home in the suburbs, she had jumped at it. Though they had good times in the big city, coming back home to the close-knit community she was familiar with was her dream for raising a family. With time, she had fallen totally in love with the practicality of it all. Here, they could take walks when needed and the boys had plenty of room to play as they explored the landscape and enjoyed the sandy beaches. It wasn't called one of the most beautiful places in the world for nothing.

Celia unlocked the Subaru station wagon, and the boys jumped into the back seats.

"Seatbelts!" Celia said.
"Check!" the boys replied out of sync as they frantically hurried to belt up.

Celia was about to switch on the car when she realized she had forgotten the bag of beauty products in the house. They were crucial to her daily run of driving around to meet clients, make deliveries and offer her expertise as a beauty consultant.

"Oh, drat," she whispered under her breath.

"Oh, drat!" James parroted back gleefully.

Celia turned back to look at him. His smile almost disarmed her again, but she needed to draw a line here.

"What did we say about talking back to mommy?"

"Don't talk back unless you ask us a question," James replied.

"Good. Let's keep it that way, okay?" she said, smiling. James nodded. Celia hoped she wouldn't have to do that very often.

"All right guys, let's get back out."

"Why?" James asked.

"Mommy forgot her products in the house. Come on, I need a pair of strong hands," she said as she got out of the car.

The kids followed her to the house.

 A few years ago, Celia would have left the boys in the car–what harm would a thirty second wait do? A lot. Celia had once made them wait in the car as she went back for something she had forgotten. When she returned, she found a scruffy, strange man walking up to the car. She screamed her lungs out, and he took off. Trevor, who was home that morning, came out with a gun. Since then, they resolved to always keep the boys close, and Celia wasn't about to drop the ball on that one.

She got the bag of beauty products without much ado, and they walked back to the car. Celia rarely forgot things, and when she did, she knew it could be a sign of exhaustion. It had been an intense couple of weeks running the business and a whole household with two energetic boys. As she fought to keep her wits sharp, she wished Trevor was around to help her.

"What's drat, Mom?" James asked. They were at the front courtyard of the school.

"Well, in the evening, when you tell me all the good things that will happen in school today, I'll also tell you what that is. Deal?" Celia said. James nodded. She hugged both of her sons and watched them walk up the steps and into the school building.

Celia headed back to the spot where she had parked her car and got in. Instead of driving off, she took a moment to do something that was becoming a habit: people watching. Looking on as parents dropped off their children, Celia narrowed her focus to the mothers.

Some women were office workers who needed to drop off their kids before embarking on the half-hour drive to the city center. Celia liked their trim outfits that suited the corporate office spaces they worked in. Some had office access tags hanging off their necks because they would only have seconds to race into their offices before their bosses raised hell. Savvy!

The other group appeared to be housewives. They were the ones who always had no urgency to their drop off routine; many would seek to do the final touches to their kids' uniforms while in the parking lot. They would also have separate lunch boxes for their kids and take the longest to say goodbye. Cute!

Watching both groups in action, Celia figured she was somewhere in the middle. She had the urgency and focus of the office-going women, and the motherly care and flexibility of the housewives.

She took out her notebook and looked through the list of client deliveries she needed to make. It was a day full of back-to-back deliveries, and she resolved that if it got too hectic, she would readjust her schedule and add an afternoon siesta to the mix.

First on the list was Christine Owens, a seventy-year-old feisty woman who lived close by. She had been a good client initially, but her enthusiasm for prompt payment had recently been replaced with an indifference that Celia didn't like. Celia didn't run her business on credit, but had made an exception with Mrs. Owens on her last delivery because she was a good family friend. Since then, it had been hard to get Mrs. Owens to pay up.

Maybe it was time for a change in approach.

The Macan Residences was a quiet, semi-posh residential neighborhood full of robust, identikit bungalows. A lot of older residents with a decent bit of money lived there, forming a crucial community of peers who supported each other as they lived through their sunset years. The relative affluence of the place made Celia wonder why Mrs. Owens wouldn't pay her dues.

Mrs. Owens' house was at the corner of the street. It had blue highlights to its cream walls and red-tiled roof, something Celia found odd but couldn't judge harshly. She rationalized that it could be a pricey blue color only found in Italy, perhaps, because sometimes what you think is tacky is rare and classy in other quarters.

After she parked along the street next to the house, Celia picked a small little gift bag labeled 'Maven Beauty Treats' from the passenger seat. She walked to the front door and gave it three confident knocks.

Nothing.

Celia knocked again, a little louder. Still no response.

She peeped through the glass in the door and, beyond the transparent lace curtain, she saw the form of Mrs. Owens lying on the floor, face up. She wasn't moving. Celia could hear a faint sound seep through - it sounded like music.

Celia's hand started shaking. She was getting anxious wondering if Mrs. Owens was just unconscious or, God forbid the thought, dead.

Makeup
and
Mayhem
SUNSHINE COVE COZY MYSTERY
AVA ZUMA

ALSO BY AVA ZUMA

The Sunny Cove Cozy Mystery Series

Makeup and Mayhem (Book 1)

Eyebrows and Evil Looks (Book 2)

New Nails and a Nasty Nightmare (Book 3)